Tales Told By Balebos And Gusan

Traditional tales, fables and sagas

from the Eastern Mediterranean ...

Compiled, Adapted & Edited by Clive Gilson

Tales from the World's Firesides

Book 3 in Part 4 of the series: The Middle East

Tales Told By Balebos And Gusan, edited by Clive Gilson, Solitude, Bath, UK

www.clivegilson.com

First print edition © 2024, Clive Gilson

Printed by IngramSpark

ISBN: 978-1-915081-22-3

I have edited Clive Gilson's books for over a decade now – he's prolific and can turn his hand to many genres. poetry, short fiction, contemporary novels, folklore, and science fiction – and the common theme is that none of them ever fails to take my breath away. There's something in each story that is either memorably poignant, hauntingly unnerving, or sidesplittingly funny.

Lorna Howarth, *The Write Factor*

Tales From The World's Firesides is a grand project. I've collected '000's of traditional texts as part of other projects, and while many of the original texts are available through channels like Project Gutenberg, some of the narratives can be hard to read by modern readers, & so the Fireside project was born. Put simply, I collect, collate & adapt traditional tales from around the world & publish them as a modern archive. *Part 1* covers a host of nations & regions across Europe. I'm not laying any claim to insight or specialist knowledge, but these collections are born out of my love of storytelling & I hope that you'll share my affection for traditional tales, myths & legends.

Chapter image by Bumiputra from Pixabay

Cover image by Septimiu Balica from Pixabay

ORIGINAL FICTION BY CLIVE GILSON

- Songs of Bliss
- Out of the Walled Garden
- The Mechanic's Curse
- The Insomniac Booth
- A Solitude of Stars

AS EDITOR – *FIRESIDE TALES – Part 1, Europe*

- Tales From the Land of Dragons
- Tales From the Land of The Brave
- Tales From the Land of Saints And Scholars
- Tales From the Land of Hope And Glory
- Tales From Lands of Snow and Ice
- Tales From the Viking Isles
- Tales From the Forest Lands
- Tales From the Old Norse
- More Tales About Saints and Scholars
- More Tales About Hope and Glory
- More Tales About Snow and Ice
- Tales From the Land of Rabbits
- Tales Told by Bulls and Wolves
- Tales of Fire and Bronze
- Tales From the Land of the Strigoi
- Tales Told by the Wind Mother
- Tales from Gallia
- Tales from Germania

EDITOR – *FIRESIDE TALES – Part 2, North America*

- Okaraxta - Tales from The Great Plains
- Tibik-Kìzis – Tales from The Great Lakes & Canada
- Jóhonaa'éí –Tales from America's Southwest
- QugaaĝiX̂ - First Nation Tales from Alaska & The Arctic
- Karahkwa - First Nation Tales from America's Eastern States
- Pot-Likker - Folklore, Fairy Tales, and Settler Stories from America

EDITOR – *FIRESIDE TALES – Part 3, Africa*

- Arokin Tales – Folklore & Fairy Tales from West Africa
- Hadithi Tales – Folklore & Fairy Tales from East Africa
- Inkathaso Tales – Folklore & Fairy Tales from Southern Africa
- Tarubadur Tales – Folklore & Fairy Tales from North Africa
- Elephant And Frog – Folklore from Central Africa

CONTENTS

Preface

I've been collecting and telling stories for a couple of decades now, having had several of my own fictional works published in recent years. My particularly focus is on short story writing in the realms of magical realities and science fiction fantasies.

I've always drawn heavily on traditional folk and fairy tales, and in so doing have amassed a collection of many thousands of these tales from around the world. It has been one of my long-standing ambitions to gather these stories together and to create a library of tales that tell the stories of places and peoples around the world.

One of the main motivations for me in undertaking the project is to collect and tell stories that otherwise might be lost or, at best, be forgotten. Given that a lot of my sources are from early collectors, particularly covering works produced in the late eighteenth century, throughout the nineteenth century, and in the early years of the twentieth century, I do make every effort to adapt stories for a modern reader. Early collectors had a different world view to many of us today, and often expressed views about race and gender, for example, that we find difficult to reconcile in the early years of the twenty-first century. I try, although with varying degrees of success, to update these stories with sensitivity while trying to stay as true to the original spirit of each story as I can.

I also want to assure readers that I try hard not to comment on or appropriate originating cultures. It is almost certainly true that the early collectors of these tales, with their then prevalent world views, have made assumptions about the originating cultures that have given us these tales. I hope that you'll accept my mission to preserve these tales, however and wherever I find them, as just that. I have, therefore, made sure that every story has a full attribution, covering both the original collector / writer and the collection title that this version has been adapted from, as well as having notes about publishers and other relevant and, I hope, interesting source data. Wherever possible I have added a cultural or indigenous attribution as well, although for some of the titles, the country-based theme is obvious.

This volume, *Tales Told By Balebos And Gusan*, is the third in a set of collections covering indigenous tales from what we know now as The Middle East. *Tales Told By Balebos And Gusan* traces the arc of storytelling across countries that we are familiar with such as Palestine, Syria, Lebanon, Jordan and Israel. In particular, this volume also reaches into the ancient Armenian tradition of storytelling, which is an absolute delight.

The title of this collection is based on the Yiddish and Armenian words for storyteller. A Yiddish storyteller is often referred to as a *balebos*, which roughly translates to "master of the house" or "head of the household" in Yiddish. This term is used to denote someone who is skilled at telling stories, particularly within the context of Jewish culture and tradition. In Yiddish-speaking communities, storytelling has long been a cherished tradition, with balebosim passing down tales of folklore, history, and morality from one generation to the next. These storytellers play a vital role in preserving and transmitting the rich oral heritage of Yiddish-speaking communities.

In Armenian culture, a storyteller is often referred to as a *gusan* (qnւսան) or *gusano* (qnւսանn), which translates to "bard" or "minstrel." The gusan tradition is deeply rooted in Armenian history and folklore, with storytellers playing a significant role in preserving and transmitting Armenian oral traditions, epic poems, historical narratives, and folk tales. These storytellers are revered for their ability to captivate audiences with their tales, often accompanied by musical instruments such as the duduk or the kamancha. They serve as custodians of Armenian cultural heritage, passing down stories from generation to generation and embodying the spirit of Armenian identity and resilience.

Jewish folk and fairy tales are unique in several ways, reflecting the cultural and religious heritage of the Jewish people. Jewish folktales often incorporate themes and motifs from Jewish religious texts, such as the Torah and the Talmud, as well as from Jewish customs, traditions, and folklore. These stories often reflect Jewish values, ethics, and beliefs, offering moral lessons and insights into Jewish identity and culture.

It is also the case that Jewish folktales have been influenced by the diverse cultural and geographical contexts in which Jewish communities have lived throughout history. As a result, these tales may feature elements borrowed from the folklore of other cultures, including Eastern European, Middle Eastern, and Mediterranean traditions.

Like many folk traditions, Jewish folktales have been passed down orally from generation to generation, evolving and adapting over time as they are retold by storytellers. This oral tradition has contributed to the richness and diversity of Jewish folk narrative, with variations of stories appearing in different regions and communities.

As with most traditions, Jewish folk and fairy tales often include supernatural elements, such as magic, demons, angels, and miracles. These fantastical elements are used to explore themes of faith, destiny, and the divine, and to entertain and inspire listeners.

While Jewish folk and fairy tales are rooted in Jewish culture and tradition, they also address universal themes and experiences that resonate with people of all backgrounds. These themes may include love, friendship, justice, redemption, and the struggle between good and evil.

Overall, Jewish folk and fairy tales offer a rich tapestry of storytelling that reflects the complexities and diversity of Jewish life and thought. They serve not only as entertainment but also as a means of transmitting values, preserving cultural heritage, and fostering a sense of belonging within the Jewish community.

When we consider the Armenian tradition, we find that Armenian folk and fairy tales are also rich with unique cultural and historical elements that distinguish them from tales of other cultures.

Armenian folktales often reflect the history, customs, and traditions of the Armenian people, including their experiences as an ancient civilization, their struggles for independence, and their rich cultural heritage.

In terms of influences, Armenian folk and fairy tales are clearly influenced by both pagan mythology and Christian beliefs. Many stories incorporate elements from Armenian mythology, such as gods, goddesses, and mythical creatures, as well as Christian themes and symbols, such as saints, angels, and miracles.

Like many folk traditions, Armenian folktales often convey moral lessons and values, such as honesty, courage, kindness, and loyalty. These tales serve as a means of teaching ethical principles and guiding behaviour within Armenian society.

Like their Jewish counterparts, Armenian folk and fairy tales have been passed down orally from generation to generation, with storytellers preserving and retelling these tales through spoken word. This oral tradition has contributed to the diversity and richness of Armenian folklore, with variations of stories appearing in different regions and communities.

Armenian folk and fairy tales often contain symbolic elements and allegorical themes, which are used to convey deeper truths and insights about life, human nature, and the world. These symbols may include animals, plants, natural phenomena, and supernatural beings, each carrying layers of meaning and significance.

Armenian folk and fairy tales have been influenced by the experiences and traditions of Armenian communities living outside of Armenia, particularly in regions such as the Middle East, Europe, and the Americas. As a result, Armenian folklore exhibits a diversity of themes, motifs, and storytelling styles.

For me, Armenian folk and fairy tales offer a glimpse into the unique cultural identity and worldview of the Armenian people, celebrating their history, values, and resilience through the art of storytelling.

These titles will grow over coming years to tell lost and forgotten tales from every continent, and even then, I'll just be scratching the surface of the world's lore and love. That's the great gift in storytelling. Since the first of our ancestors sat around in a cave, contemplating an ape's place in the world, we have, as a species, told each other stories of magic and cunning and caution and love. When I began to read through tales from the Celts, tales from Indonesia, tales from Africa and the Far East, tales from everywhere, one of the things that struck me clearly was just how similar are our roots. We share characters and characteristics. The nature of these tales is so similar underneath the local camouflage. Human beings clearly share a storytelling heritage so much deeper than the world that we see superficially as always having been just as it is now.

These tales were originally told by firelight as a way of preserving histories and educating both adult and child. These tales form part of our shared heritage, witches, warts, fantastic beasts, and all. They can be dark and violent. They can be sweet and loving. They are we and we are they in so many ways. I've loved reading and re-reading these stories. I hope you do too.

Clive

Bath

February 2024

The Golden Maiden

This story has been adapted from Abraham G. Seklemian's version of the same tale that originally appeared in The Golden Maiden and Other Folk Tales and Fairy Stories Told in Armenia, published in 1898 by The Helman-Taylor Company, New York. This tale is based on earlier work undertaken by Ohannes Chatschumian, who, before his death, had begun a compilation of 'Armenian' folklore for Miss Alice Fletcher. These 'Armenian' tales themselves originated in the Byzantine peasant tradition that developed over the preceding fifteen hundred years.

Once upon a time there was a wicked widow who had an ugly daughter. She married a second husband who had a beautiful daughter and a son by his first wife. The step-mother hated the two motherless children, and used every means to persuade her husband to take them away to the mountains and abandon them as a prey to wild beasts. The poor man loved his children, but being frail was unable to resist the frequent importunities and threats made by his wife. Therefore one day he put bread in a bag, and taking the two children went to the mountains. After a long journey they came to a lonely wilderness.

The man then said to the children, "Sit here and take a little rest," and then, turning his face away, he began to sob bitterly.

"Father, father, why are you weeping?" exclaimed the children, and they also began to weep.

The man opened the bag and gave them bread, which they soon ate.

"Father," said the boy, "I am thirsty."

The man drove his stick into the ground, and placing his cloak over the stick, said, "Come, children, sit here under the shadow of this cloak. I will go and see if there is a fountain nearby."

The children seated themselves under the cloak, while their father disappeared behind the trees and rocks.

After waiting a long time, the two innocent children grew tired and began to ramble about in search of their father, but in vain.

"Father, father!" they exclaimed, but only the echo of the mountains returned them answer - "Father, father!"

The children came back, crying, "Alas, alas! The stick is here, the cloak is here, but father is not here!"

Thus they cried for a long time, but seeing that nobody appeared, they rose up, and one of them took the stick and the other the cloak and they began to wander about in the wilderness, not knowing where to go. After a long ramble, they came to a place where some rain-water had gathered on the ground in a print made by the hoof of a horse.

"Sister," said the little boy, "I am thirsty; I want to drink this water."

"No," said the maiden, "do not drank this water. As soon as you drink it you will become a colt."

Soon they came to another print made by the hoof of an ox, and the boy said, "Sister, I am thirsty and I want to drink."

But she would not let him drink, saying, "As soon as you drink this water you will become a calf."

Then they came to another print made by the paw of a bear, and the boy wanted to drink; but his sister prevented him in case he should become a cub of a bear. Then they came to a track made by the foot of a pig, and the boy again wanted to drink, but the maiden prevented him, in case he should turn into a young pig. Soon they came to a print made by the foot of a wolf, but the boy did not give in to his thirst until they came to a puddle made by the hoof of a lamb.

"Sister," exclaimed the boy, "I am thirsty. I cannot wait any longer; I will drink from this at any risk."

"Alas," said the maiden, "what can I do? I am ready to give my life to save you, but it is impossible. You will turn into a lamb the moment you drink this water."

The boy drank, and was at once changed into a lamb, and began to follow his sister bleating. After a long and dangerous journey they found the way to the town, and came to their house. The step-mother was angry to see them come back, even though one of them was now a lamb.

She had great influence over her husband, and he used every means at his disposal to please her. One day she said to him, "I want to eat meat. You must kill your lamb that I may eat it."

The sister, hearing this, at once took her lamb-brother and fled secretly to the mountains, where, sitting on a high rock, she spun wool while the lamb grazed safely near her. As she was spinning, her spindle fell suddenly from her hand, and fell into a deep cave. The maiden, leaving the lamb grazing, went down to find her spindle. Entering the cave, she was surprised to see an old fairy woman, a dame a thousand years of age, who perceiving the maiden, exclaimed, "Maiden, neither the bird with its wing, nor the snake on its belly can enter here. How could you venture to come here?"

The terrified maiden was at a loss for an answer, but she replied with a gentle voice, "Your love brought me here, grandmother."

The old fairy was pleased with this kind answer, and calling the maiden, gave her a seat beside herself and asked her many things concerning the upper world. The more she talked with the maiden the better she liked her and she said, "Now you are hungry. Let me bring you some fishes to eat."

She went into the cave, and returned with a plateful of cooked snakes, at the sight of which the maiden shuddered with horror and began to weep.

"What is the matter?" inquired the old dame, "Why are you weeping?"

"Nothing at all," answered the maiden, shyly, "I remembered my dead mother who was so fond of fish, and therefore I wept."

Then she told the old dame her sad story, and the ill treatment of the wicked step-mother. The fairy woman was very much interested in what the maiden told her, and said to her, "Be seated and let me sleep in your lap. In yonder fireplace there is a ploughshare heated in the fire. When the Black Fairy passes do not waken me; but when the Red-and-Green Fairy passes, press the red-hot ploughshare on my feet at once so that I may wake up."

The poor maiden shuddered with fear, but she could do nothing but consent. Accordingly the old fairy woman lay down in the maiden's lap and slept. Soon a fairy as black as night passed through the cave, but the maiden did not stir. After him the Red-and-Green Fairy appeared and the whole cave was gilded with his radiant beams. The maiden at once pressed the red-hot ploughshare on the feet of the sleeping fairy woman, who immediately started up exclaiming, "Oh! What is biting my feet?"

The maiden told her that nothing had bitten her, but it was the red-hot ploughshare she felt, and that it was time to get up. The old dame arose and at once caused the maiden to stand up as the Red-and-Green Fairy proceeded, whose gleaming rays had such an effect upon her that her hair and garments were all turned to gold and she herself was turned into a fairy maiden. After the Red-and-Green Fairy disappeared, the maiden, kissing the fairy woman's hand, took leave of her, and taking her lamb-brother, went home. Seeing that the step-mother was not at home, she at once took off her golden garments and hiding them in a secret corner, put on her old rags.

Soon the step-mother entered, and seeing the golden hair of the maiden, exclaimed, "How now, little elf! What did you do to your hair to turn it into gold?"

The maiden told her what had taken place. On the following day the step-mother sent her own daughter to the same spot. There, on purpose, she let her spindle fall, and entered the cave as if to pick it up. The fairy woman saw her, and taking a dislike to her, changed her into an ugly thing, so ugly that it is impossible to describe her appearance. She came home, and the step-mother seeing her own daughter changed into a form of so great ugliness, was the more enraged against the two step-children.

One day the Prince of that country sent out heralds to proclaim all over his realm that his son was to be married, and that the most beautiful maiden in all the land should be his bride. He commanded all the marriageable maidens to assemble in the palace courtyard where the young Prince would make his selection. At the appointed time all the maidens of the land had crowded into the courtyard. The step-mother dressed her own daughter in the best garments and ornaments she could procure, veiling her ugly face very carefully, however, and took her to the courtyard, hoping that the Prince would select her for his bride. In order to prevent the orphan maiden from appearing before the Prince, the step-mother scattered a measure of wheat in the yard, and bade the maiden to pick up the wheat before she returned, threatening to beat her to death if she failed to finish the task. Soon after the step-mother went away, however, the maiden let loose the chickens, which in a moment picked the wheat up to the very last grain. She put on her golden garments and was changed to a fairy maiden so beautiful that she might say to the sun, "Sun, you need not shine, for I am shining."

Then she went to the Prince's courtyard, where she was the object of the admiration of all the crowd. But she could not stay very long in case her step-mother should return first, and not finding her at home should beat her upon her return, so she ran hastily back, and hiding her golden garments put on her old rags. But in her haste she had dropped one of her golden slippers in the Prince's fountain.

Soon the young Prince, who had looked at the maidens without making a selection, came on horseback leading his animal to the fountain to water him, but the horse was frightened by the radiant beams from the slipper. The servants immediately entered the fountain, and taking out the slipper gave it to the prince, who seeing it at once declared that the maiden who wore that slipper should be his bride. He and his peers began to search every house and to try the feet of the maidens to find the true owner of the slipper. They had just approached the house of the Golden Maiden, when the stepmother took her and hid her in the great kitchen pit which is used as a furnace, presenting her own ugly daughter as the owner of the golden slipper. Of course, the slipper did not fit. As the Prince and his peers were leaving the house, the cock flying from his roost perched on the top of the door, and cried, "Goo-goo-lig-goo-goo! The Golden Maiden is in the pit!"

The pit was immediately opened, and the maiden jumped out. The slipper fitted, and the maiden, taking out her golden garments and the mate of the slipper from the corner where she had hidden them, put them on, and was changed to a fairy maiden. The Prince seeing this embraced her as his bride. Taking the lamb-brother with them, they went to the Prince's palace, where their nuptials were celebrated for seven days and seven nights.

One day the step-mother took her own daughter and went to the Prince's palace to pay a visit to her step-daughter, who conducted them to the Prince's orchard for a walk. As they came to the seashore the step-mother said, "Come, daughters, let us take a bath in the sea."

No sooner had they entered the sea, than the step-mother, intending to drown the golden bride, pushed her into the deep water. A great fish, however, chanced to be there and swallowed her. The step-mother at once gathered up the golden dresses of the bride, and putting them on her own ugly daughter, brought her to the palace. There she left her in the place of the golden bride, carefully veiling her ugly face.

The true bride remained in the fish's belly for some days. One day, early in the morning, she heard the sexton ringing the bell and inviting people to church. She cried to him from the belly of the fish:

"Sexton! Sexton! Who ring your morning bell,

Crossing your face, send the devils to hell,

For God's sake, go to the young Prince and tell,

Let him not kill my lamb-brother or sell."

The sexton, hearing this call repeated several times, went and informed the young Prince, who had by that time discovered the loss of his fairy bride. He immediately came to the seashore, where the sexton had heard the voice. Once more it was repeated, and the Prince recognized it as the voice of his bride. He drew his sword and leaped into the sea. Splitting the fish's belly, he drew out his bride, and taking her in his arms brought her to the palace. Soon he called the step-mother before him, saying, "Now, kind mother, which gift do you prefer, a nimble-footed horse or a keen sword?"

"Let your keen sword stab your enemies," answered the step-mother, overjoyed with the expectation of a valuable present, "I will have the nimble-footed horse."

"I take you at your word," said the Prince, "you shall have the horse."

He ordered his men to bind the step-mother and her ugly daughter to the tail of a wild horse. It was done, and the horse being whipped, carried the two wicked women away to the mountains. They were thrown from stone to stone, and from tree to tree, until they were dashed into pieces.

The wicked persons being punished, the Prince celebrated a new nuptial for forty days and forty nights, because he had found his lost golden bride. She, being released from her rival, thenceforth enjoyed a happy life with her lamb-brother.

The Palace Of The Eagles

This story has been adapted from Gertrude Landa's version of the same tale that originally appeared in Jewish Fairy Tales and Legends, published in 1943 by Bloch Publishing Co. Inc., New York.

East of the Land of the Rising Sun there dwelled a king who spent all his days and half his nights in pleasure. His kingdom was on the edge of the world, according to the knowledge of those times, and almost entirely surrounded by the sea. Nobody seemed to care what lay beyond the barrier of rocks that shut off the land from the rest of the world. For the matter of that, nobody appeared to trouble much about anything in that kingdom.

Most of the people followed the example of the king and led idle, careless lives, giving no thought to the future. The king regarded the task of governing his subjects as a big nuisance. He did not care to be worried with proposals concerning the welfare of the masses, and documents brought to him by his advisors for signature were never read. For all he knew they may have referred to the school regulations of the moon, instead of the laws of trading and such like public matters.

"Don't bother me," was his usual remark. "You are my advisors and officers of state. Deal with affairs as you think best."

And off he would go to his beloved hunting which was his favourite pastime.

The land was fertile, and nobody had ever entertained an idea that bad weather might some year affect the crops and cause a scarcity of grain. They took no precautions to lay in stocks of wheat, and so when one summer there was a great lack of rain and the fields were parched, the winter that followed was marked by suffering. The kingdom was faced by famine, and the people did not like it. They did not know what to do, and when they appealed to the king, he could not help them. Indeed, he could not understand the difficulty.

He passed it off very lightly. "I am a mighty hunter," he said. "I can always kill enough beasts to provide a sufficiency of food."

But the drought had withered away the grass and the trees, and the shortage of such food had greatly reduced the number of animals. The king found the forests empty of deer and birds. Still he failed to realize the gravity of the situation and what he considered an exceedingly bright idea struck him.

"I will explore the unknown territory beyond the barrier of rocky hills," he said. "Surely there I will find a land of plenty. And, at least" he added, "it will be a pleasant adventure with good hunting."

A great expedition was therefore arranged, and the king and his hunting companions set forth to find a path over the rocks. This was not at all difficult, and on the third day, a pass was discovered among the crags and peaks that formed the summit of the barrier, and the king saw the region beyond.

It seemed a vast and beautiful land, stretching away as far as the eye could see in a forest of huge trees. Carefully, the hunters descended the other side of the rock barrier and entered the unknown land.

It seemed uninhabited. Nor was there any sign of beast or bird of any kind. No sound disturbed the stillness of the forest, no tracks were visible. As well as the hunters could make out, no foot had ever trodden the region before. Even nature seemed at rest. The trees were all old, their trunks gnarled into fantastic shapes, their leaves yellow and sere as if growth had stopped ages ago.

Altogether the march through the forest was rather eerie, and the hunters proceeded in single file, which added to the impressiveness of the strange experience. The novelty, however, made it pleasant to the king, and he kept on his way for four days.

Then the forest ended abruptly, and the explorers came to a vast open plain, a desert, through which a wide river flowed. Far beyond rose a mountain capped by rocks of regular shape. At any rate, they appeared to be rocks, but the distance was too great to enable anyone to speak with certainty.

"Water," said the vizier, "is a sign of life."

So the king decided to continue as far as the mountain. A ford was discovered in the river, and once on the other side it was possible to make out the rocks crowning the mountain. They looked too regular to be mere rocks, and on approaching nearer the king was sure that a huge building must be at the top of the mountain. When they arrived quite close, there was no doubt about it. Either a town, or a palace, stood on the summit, and it was decided to make the ascent next day.

During the night no sound was heard, but to everybody's surprise a distinct path up the mountain was noticed in the morning. It was so overgrown with weeds and moss and straggling creepers that it was obvious it had not been used for a long time. The ascent was accordingly difficult, but halfway up the first sign of life, noticed since the expedition began, made itself visible.

It was an eagle. Suddenly it flew down from the mountain top and circled above the hunters, screaming, but making no attempt to attack.

At length the summit was gained. It was a flat plateau of great expanse, almost the whole of which was covered by an enormous building of massive walls and stupendous towers.

"This is the palace of a great monarch," said the king.

But no entrance of any kind could be seen. The rest of the day was spent in wandering round, but nowhere could they find a door, or window, or opening. It was decided to make a more serious effort to gain entry the next morning.

However, it seemed a greater puzzle than ever. At length, one of the most venturesome of the party discovered an eagle's nest on one of the smallest towers, and with great difficulty he secured the bird and brought it down to the king. His majesty bade one of his wise men, Muflog, learned in bird languages, to speak to it. He did so.

In a harsh croaking voice, the eagle replied, "I am but a young bird, only seven centuries old. I know nothing. On a tower higher than that on which I dwell, is the eyrie of my father. He may be able to give you information."

The eagle would say no more. The only thing to do was to climb the higher tower and question the father eagle. This was done, and the bird answered, "On a tower still higher dwells my father, and on yet a higher tower my grandfather, who is two thousand years old. He may know something. I know nothing."

After considerable difficulty the topmost tower was reached and the venerable bird discovered. He seemed asleep and was only awakened after much coaxing. Then he surveyed the hunters warily.

"Let me see, let me think," he muttered slowly. "I did hear, when I was a tiny eagle chick, but a few years old - that was long, long ago - that my great-grandfather had said that his great-grandfather had told him he had heard that long, long, long ago - oh, ever so much longer than that - a king lived in this palace. They said that he died and left it to the eagles, and that in the course of many, many, many thousands of years the door had been covered up by the dust brought by the winds."

"Where is the door?" asked Muflog.

That was a puzzle the ancient bird could not answer readily. He thought and thought and fell asleep and had to be kept being awakened until at last he remembered.

"When the sun shines in the morning," he croaked, "its first ray falls on the door." Then, worn out with all his thinking and talking, he fell asleep again.

There was no rest for the party that night. They all watched to make certain of seeing the first ray of the rising sun strike the palace. When it did so, the spot was carefully noted. But no door could be seen. Digging was therefore begun and after many hours, an opening was found.

Through this an entrance was made into the palace. What a wonderful and mysterious place it was, all overgrown with the weeds of centuries! Tangled masses of creepers lay everywhere-- over what were once trimly kept pathways, and almost completely hiding the lower buildings. In the crevices of the walls, roots had insinuated themselves, and by their growth had forced the stones apart. It was all a terrible scene of desolation. The king's men had to hack a path laboriously through the wilderness of weeds with their swords before they could reach the central building, and when they did so they came to a door on which an inscription was cut deep into the wood. The language was unknown to all but Muflog, who deciphered it as follows, "We, the Dwellers in this Palace, lived for many years in Comfort and Luxury. Then Hunger came. We had made no preparation. We had amassed jewels in abundance but not Corn. We ground Pearls and Rubies to fine flour, but could make no Bread. So, we die, bequeathing this Palace to the eagles who will devour our bodies and build their eyries on our towers."

A dread silence fell on the whole party when Muflog read these strange words, and the king turned pale. This warning from the dead past was making the adventure far from enjoyable. Some of the party suggested the immediate abandonment of the expedition and the prompt return home. They feared hidden dangers now. But the king remained resolute.

"I must investigate this to the end," he said in a firm voice. "Those who are seized by fear may return. I will go on, if needs be, alone."

Encouraged by these words, the hunters decided to remain with the king. One of them began to batter at the door, but the king was anxious to preserve the inscription, and after more cutting away of weeds, the key was seen to be sticking in the keyhole. Unlocking the door, however, was no light task, for ages of rust had accumulated. When finally this was accomplished the door creaked heavily on its hinges and a musty smell came from the dank corridor that was revealed.

The explorers walked ankle-deep in dust through a maze of rooms until they came to a big central hall of statues. So artistically fashioned were they that they seemed lifelike in their attitudes, and for a moment all held their breath. This hall was dustless, and Muflog pointed out that it was an airtight chamber. Evidently it had been specifically devised to preserve the statues.

"These must be the effigies of kings," said his majesty, and on reading the inscriptions, Muflog said that was so.

At the far end of the hall, on a pedestal higher than the others, was a statue bigger than the rest. In addition to the name there was an inscription on the pedestal. Muflog read it amid an awed stillness.

"I am the last of the kings - the last of men - and with my own hands have completed this work. I ruled over a thousand cities, rode on a thousand horses, and received the homage of a thousand vassal princes, but when Famine came I was powerless. You who may read this, take heed of the fate that has overwhelmed this land. Take but one word of counsel from the last of the mortals. Prepare your meal while the daylight lasts…"

The words broke off, for the rest was undecipherable.

"Enough," cried the king, and his voice was not steady. "This has indeed been good hunting. I have learned, in my folly and pursuit of pleasure, what I had failed to see for myself. Let us return and act upon the counsel of this king who has met the end that will surely be our own should we forget his warning."

Looking out across the plain they had traversed, his majesty seemed to see a vision of prosperous cities and smiling fertile fields. In imagination, he saw caravans laden with merchandise journeying across the intervening spaces. Then, as darker thoughts followed, a cloud appeared to settle over the whole land. The cities crumbled and disappeared, the eagles swooped down and took possession of that which man had failed to appreciate and hold. After the eagles the dust of the ages settled slowly, piling itself up year by year until everything was covered and only the desert was visible.

Scarcely a word was spoken as the king and his hunters made their way back to the land East of the Rising Sun. In all, they had been away forty days when they re-crossed the barrier of rocks. They were joyously welcomed.

"What have you brought," asked the populace. "In a little while we shall be starving."

"You shall not starve," said the king. "I have brought wisdom from the Palace of the Eagles. From the fate and sufferings of others I have learned a lesson - my duty."

At once he set to work to organize the proper distribution of the food supply and the cultivation of the land. He wasted no more time on foolish pleasures, and in due course the land East of the Rising Sun enjoyed happiness and prosperity and even established fruitful colonies in the plain overlooked by the Palace of the Eagles.

Og, King Of Bashan

This story has been adapted from Henry Wysham Lanier's version of the same tale that originally appeared in A Book of Giants, published in 1922 by E. P. Dutton and Company, New York.

The Hebrew chroniclers tell us that the giants of their land were the children of the fallen angels who took to themselves wives from the beautiful daughters of men. When these huge beings had consumed the possessions of their neighbours, they began to devour even the human beings themselves, and from this horrible example men came to kill and eat birds, animals and fishes.

Of these terrific and wicked ones, merely to glance at whom made one's heart grow weak, the most celebrated was Og. His mother Enac was a daughter of Adam. Like all of his race he was by nature half mortal, for being part angel, part human, these monsters, after a very long life, found themselves with but half a body, the rest having withered away. With the prospect of remaining forever in this uncomfortable state, they were wont either to plunge into the sea or to end this miserable half existence by means of a magic herb, the secret of which had been transmitted by their celestial ancestors. Og, however, was destined, in this as in other matters, for a different fate from that of his brethren.

When the wickedness and arrogance of the Cainites brought the Flood upon the earth, Noah, as commanded, gathered his family and the animals into the ark he had built. All the rest of the miserable folk perished in the waters - with the single exception of the giant Og. The latter had persuaded Noah to save him by promising that he and his descendants would in return serve the family of Noah forever. But when they came to embark, it was discovered that the vessel was not large enough to accommodate this huge creature, so he was permitted to sit on top of the ark, and during those weary months when the waters covered the face of the earth, those within passed food to the giant through a hole in the roof.

There are, indeed, writers who declare that Og escaped because his stature was such that the deluge at its deepest reached only to his knees, he being accustomed to drink water direct from the clouds. In fact, Abba Saul says, "I once hunted a stag which fled into the thigh-bone of a dead man. I pursued it and ran for nearly eight miles of the thigh-bone, yet had not yet reached its end" - and this bone proved to be a portion of Og's skeleton. In Moses' time, however, the giant's great iron-bedstead was a mere thirteen or fourteen feet long. Whatever his height, his breadth was half as great, instead of only one-third as in the normal man.

There was also one animal too large to enter the ark, the reëm or unicorn. It was therefore tied to the stern and "ran on behind." Undoubtedly this difficult mode of travelling proved fatal since we have no authentic record of that beast since then.

Og had better fortune. Whether wading or bestriding the vessel, he won through, for we find him again some hundreds of years later as the slave of Abraham, to whom he had been presented by Nimrod. Finally, after these centuries of servitude, his master freed him as a reward for bringing back Rebekah as a bride for his son Isaac.

God also rewarded him in this world, that this wicked wight might not lay claim to a reward in the world to come. He therefore made a king of him.

He had also received another doubtful reward for a difficult service. Hearing that Abraham's nephew Lot had been carried away into captivity, he sped with the news, and stood by when all others were fearful, thinking in his heart that his master would hasten to his kinsman's help, and would be killed by the marauding kings, which would leave the beautiful Sarah as his own prize. Consequently he was granted another five hundred years of life, but on the conclusion of that term he was to be completely mortal.

Long did this gigantic monarch of gigantic adventures reign in Bashan, east of the Jordan River. He founded sixty walled cities, and great was his power and fame in all that land. Of his own race to the south was Sihon, King of the Amorites; and across the Dead Sea was another family of his blood, Anak and his sons and daughters. All the kings of Canaan paid tribute to Og of Bashan in return for the defence of their borders by his might. Even had he known of it, he would have been little troubled to hear that the Israelitish slaves of Pharaoh had escaped from bondage in Egypt, and were slowly moving northward through the desert towards Canaan.

Great indeed would have been his amusement had he seen the slinking spies sent out by Moses, when they reached the "City of Four" (Kiriath-Arba, or Hebron), where Anak dwelt with his mighty brood. At the mere shout of one of the sons the spies fell down as dead men, and one day the Israelites heard the Anakim roar to each other as they looked toward the trembling strangers, "There are grasshoppers by the trees that have the semblance of men."

But in spite of the timorous report of most of these scouts, the day arrived when word came to Og that this band of wanderers had defeated the Amorites, and killed Sihon and his son, and captured the impregnable city of Heshbon, and taken possession of all that region.

This brought the invaders to the very edge of Og's dominions, and when they had rested, they pressed on against the stronghold of Edrei.

Toward night they reached the outskirts, and Moses prepared to attack the following day. At dawn he rose and went forward to reconnoitre, but as he looked ahead through the greyness he cried out, "Behold, in the night they have built up a new wall about the city!"

Then the light grew gradually stronger, and he saw that what he had taken for a new fortification was the giant king himself, who sat upon the wall with his feet touching the earth.

The Israelitish host was dismayed at sight of this incredible being, who gazed upon them with scornful confidence. Even Moses himself hesitated and began to feel doubtful. Not only did ordinary weapons seem unavailing against such a prodigy, but he reflected that this giant was reputed to have lived for hundreds of years.

"Surely he could never have attained so great an age had he not performed meritorious deeds," he said to himself. He reflected too that Og was the only one of the original giant brood who had escaped the sword of the angel Amraphel, and it seemed therefore as if he must be under some sort of divine protection.

While he communed with himself and sought for guidance in prayer, he seemed to hear from on high a direct answer to his questionings.

"What does Og's gigantic stature matter to you? He is as a green leaf in your hand."

At this he took courage. Yet he could not understand in what manner he might attack the monster, since apparently no weapon he could handle would reach anywhere beyond his knees.

So he waited, considering this matter. And presently the giant stirred himself and set about bringing the issue to a close in characteristic fashion. For, noting closely the size of the encampment of the Israelites, he heaved up a huge rock, like a veritable mountain, vast enough to cover the entire camp. Bearing this upon his head, he strode forward, clearly intending to crush the entire force of his enemies at one blow.

Ill would it have fared with the band under Moses that day had they been dependent upon their own might alone. But as the giant advanced, and all waited in terror for the catastrophe, the colossal mass of rock was seen to settle down over his head. He stood still, blinded and bewildered, endeavouring to throw off this imprisoning bulk, but all his efforts were unavailing.

Then Moses, perceiving that the enemy was delivered into his hands, seized a mighty axe, and ran forward, and leaped into the air higher than an ordinary man's head, and dealt such a blow upon Og's leg that he crashed to earth with the rock on top of him.

Thus died Og, King of Bashan, last of the giants who were before the Flood. And the warriors of Israel fell upon the army which had accompanied him, and conquered it utterly, and took possession of all that land.

The Fairy Nightingale

This story has been adapted from Abraham G. Seklemian's version of the same tale that originally appeared in The Golden Maiden and Other Folk Tales and Fairy Stories Told in Armenia, published in 1898 by The Helman-Taylor Company, New York. This tale is based on earlier work undertaken by Ohannes Chatschumian, who, before his death, had begun a compilation of 'Armenian' folklore for Miss Alice Fletcher. These 'Armenian' tales themselves originated in the Byzantine peasant tradition that developed over the preceding fifteen hundred years.

A very interesting story was once told me of a King who built a splendid church. It took the architects seven years to finish the building. The King went to dedicate the church and to pray in it, and there was a fog so dense that the King was almost suffocated. In the very midst of the dense fog a monk stood before the King, saying, "Long live the King! You have built a fine church, but it lacks one thing."

The monk then quickly disappeared. The King came out and ordered his men to take down the building and to put up another one finer than the first. It took them another seven years to finish the second building. The King again went to dedicate the church and pray in it, and again there was a dense fog, and the same monk stood before the King, saying, "Long live the King! You have built a beautiful church, but it lacks one thing."

Again the monk mysteriously disappeared. The King again ordered his men to take down the building and to put up a new one. It took them another seven years to finish the third building, and it was this time so splendid that there was nothing like it in all the world. The King again went to dedicate it and to pray in it, and again there was a dense fog, and the same monk stood before the King saying, "Long live the King! You have built a church incomparably beautiful, but it lacks one thing."

The monk was again about to make his exit when the King took hold of his collar, saying, "Tell me what is the one thing lacking in my church. This is the third time that you have asked me to take down my building, upon which so much labour and time has been spent."

"The Fairy Nightingale is the only thing that is lacking in this magnificent church," said the monk, and he disappeared into the fog.

The King returned to his palace, and thereafter was very sad. He had three sons, who seeing their father sad, asked, "Long live the King! What grieves you, father?"

"My sons," said the King, "I am getting old, and the Fairy Nightingale is needed for the church. I do not know how to get it."

"Be of good cheer, father," said the lads, "we will go and bring it."

And they started. After a long journey they came to a place where the road divided into three branches, with a sign on each. The sign of the broad road was - "He who goes on this road returns safely." The sign on the middle road was - "He who goes on this road may return or may not return." And the sign on the third narrow road was - "He who goes on this road never returns."

The oldest brother took the broad road; the second brother took the middle road, and the youngest brother took the narrow road. The oldest lad soon came to a large city, at sight of which he said to himself, "Why should I go farther and be killed? I would better stay in this place." And he became a servant in one of the inns of the city.

The second brother turned toward the other side of the mountain, and came to a green meadow with shady trees here and there, and benches under the trees. He was tired, and at once sat down upon one of the benches. Soon a giant as black as night came along with an iron rod in his hand. He gave the lad one stroke with the rod, and the lad turned into a round stone, and rolled under the bench.

The youngest of the three brothers started on the road along which there could be no return. A dense fog covered him, and the monk who had talked with his father appeared to him, saying, "God speed you, son! Where are you going?"

"I am going to bring the Fairy Nightingale for our new church," said the lad.

"Good," said the monk, "but this way is dangerous, so let me advise you. The owner of the Fairy Nightingale is the Fairy Queen, a very beautiful maiden. On your way you will soon come to a river which the Fairy Queen has by her arts changed into a poisoned stream, and she does not drink from it. But you must drink from it, and say, 'Oh happy day! This is the water of immortality.' After crossing the river you will come to a grove which the queen has changed into a jungle of thorns and thistles. You must smell the trees and shrubs, and say, 'O happy day! This grove is the flower of Paradise.' Then you will come to a narrow pass on one side of which there is a wolf bound with chains, and on the other side there is a lamb bound with chains. There is a bundle of grass before the wolf, and a piece of meat before the lamb. You must put the grass before the lamb, and the meat before the wolf. You will then come to a large gate with double doors, one open and one closed. You must open the closed door and shut the open one. Entering in you will find the Fairy Queen, owner of the Fairy Nightingale, sleeping in a splendid bedchamber. She sleeps seven days and nights, and is awake seven days and nights. If you can do what I have told you, and reach there at a time when the Queen is asleep, you can bring the Nightingale; if not, you are lost."

The lad started, and came successively to the river, the grove, the lamb and the wolf, and the gate. He did all that the monk had told him, and entering in, saw an exquisite bedchamber where a maiden as beautiful as the sun was sleeping on a purple bed embroidered with gold and jewellery. The Fairy Nightingale came down from its cage, and standing on the Queen's bedside, sang to her a thousand songs with enchanting melody, and lullabied her to sound sleep. The lad, who was watching from behind the arras, seeing the maiden asleep, and that the Nightingale had returned to its cage, crept in slowly, took the Nightingale's cage, pressed a kiss upon the forehead of the sleeping maiden, thus stamping the sign of his lips there, and started back on his way.

The Queen awoke, and seeing the Nightingale had been stolen, exclaimed, "Doors, catch the thief!"

"God speed him!" said the doors, "He closed the open one of us and opened the closed one of us."

"Wolf and lamb, catch the thief!" exclaimed the Fairy Queen.

"God speed him!" said the wolf and the lamb, "He gave the meat to the wolf, and the grass to the lamb."

"Grove, catch the thief!" exclaimed the Queen.

"God speed him!" said the grove, "You made me thorns and thistles; he made me a flower of Paradise."

"River, catch the thief!" exclaimed the Queen.

"God speed him!" said the river, "You made me a stream of poison; he made me the water of immortality."

When the Queen saw that all her charms were unavailing, she mounted her horse and started in pursuit of the lad.

But let us return to the lad. He passed all the dangerous places and came to the square where the road divided into the three branches. He saw the monk waiting for him.

"Here is the Fairy Nightingale, holy father," said the lad, and seeing that his brothers had not yet come back, he give the cage to the monk and he himself started in search of his brothers. He went first along the broad road, until he came to the inn where his brother was serving. He secretly made himself known to him, and taking him away brought him to the monk. He then took the next road, and went as far as the green meadow and sat down upon one of the benches. Soon the giant appeared with his iron rod and tried to strike the lad. But the lad cleverly avoided the blow, and snatching the rod from the giant's hand, struck him. Immediately the giant fell down and was changed into a huge round black stone.

"My brother must have been lost somewhere in this place," thought the lad, and began to strike the stones scattered here and there upon the meadow with the iron rod, and the stones were changed into men, who began to run away; but his brother was not among them. He saw a stone under the bench, and struck it. It was changed into his brother, and he too began to run.

"Brother, brother, do not run, it is I," exclaimed the lad.

His brother stopped and both returned to the monk. All three, taking the Fairy Nightingale, went toward their father's city. On the way they were thirsty, and came to a well.

They lowered the youngest brother to draw water, and as soon as he reached the bottom of the well, the two older brothers said to one another, "When we go home to our father all praise and glory will be given to that fellow who is now in the well, and we shall be despised. It shall not be. He shall never come up from that well."

They cut the rope, and leaving the hero in the well, took the Nightingale and went to their father, saying, "Our youngest brother was killed in our attempt to get the Fairy Nightingale, but we two succeeded in bringing it."

They hung the cage in the new church, but the Fairy Nightingale did not warble a single song; it was sad and silent. Soon the Fairy Queen came riding to the King, and said, "Who is the hero that has brought my Nightingale?"

"We brought it," said the two brothers.

"Well, what did you meet on the way?" inquired the Queen.

"Nothing," said the lads.

"Then it was not you who brought it," said the Queen, "you are thieves." And she caused them to be arrested and cast into prison, saying, "You shall not be released until the real hero who brought the Fairy Nightingale is presented to me."

Some women who were gleaning barley in the fields happened to pass near the well where the lad was left, and hearing him groan pulled out. One of them, who had no children, adopted him as her son. After a few weeks news came from the city to the village to the effect that the King's sons had brought the Fairy Nightingale, but the

Fairy Queen, the owner of the Nightingale, also had come after it. One day the lad asked permission of his adopted mother, saying, "A new church has been built, let me go and see it."

The old woman consented, and he went to the city as a peasant boy. He went to his father's house and heard that his brothers were imprisoned. He went directly to the prison and set them free. The Fairy Queen, hearing this, came and said to the lad, "I am the Fairy Queen, the owner of the Nightingale; are you not afraid of me?"

"I am he who brought the Fairy Nightingale," said the lad, "I am not afraid of you."

"What did you see on the way?" asked the Queen.

The lad told her what he had seen and what he had done.

"And moreover," said the lad, "I have put a sign upon your forehead with my own lips. Look at your image in yonder pond, and you will see that you are my betrothed."

The Queen looked at her reflected image in the water, and seeing the mark of the lad's kiss, exclaimed, "Hero, you are worthy of me. I am yours forever."

A wedding festival for forty days and forty nights was celebrated. After this the couple went to the church to be married. The Fairy Nightingale began to warble, and sang them a thousand and one songs. It is still singing, and all the world is wondering at its sweet melodies.

The Giant Of The Flood

This story has been adapted from Gertrude Landa's version of the same tale that originally appeared in Jewish Fairy Tales and Legends, published in 1943 by Bloch Publishing Co. Inc., New York. The Giant Of The Flood is an alternative version of the tale about Og, King of Bashan.

Just before the world was drowned all the animals gathered in front of the Ark and Father Noah carefully inspected them.

"All you that lie down shall enter and be saved from the deluge that is about to destroy the world," he said. "You that stand cannot enter."

Then the various creatures began to march forward into the Ark. Father Noah watched them closely. He seemed troubled.

"I wonder," he said to himself, "how I shall obtain a unicorn, and how I shall get it into the Ark."

"I can bring you a unicorn, Father Noah," he heard in a voice of thunder, and turning round he saw the giant, Og. "But you must agree to save me, too, from the flood."

"Be gone!" cried Noah. "You are a demon, not a human being. I can have no dealings with you."

"Pity me," whined the giant. "See how my figure is shrinking. Once I was so tall that I could drink water from the clouds and toast fish at the sun. I do not fear that I shall be drowned, but that all the food will be destroyed and that I shall perish of hunger."

Noah, however, only smiled, but he grew serious again when Og brought a unicorn. It was as big as a mountain, although the giant said it was the smallest he could find. It lay down in front of the Ark and Noah saw by that action that he must save it. For some time he was puzzled what to do, but at last a bright idea struck him. He attached the huge beast to the Ark by a rope fastened to its horn so that it could swim alongside and be fed.

Og seated himself on a mountain near at hand and watched the rain pouring down. Faster and faster it fell in torrents until the rivers overflowed and the waters began to rise rapidly on the land and sweep all things away. Father Noah stood gloomily before the door of the Ark until the water reached his neck. Then it swept him inside. The door closed with a bang, and the Ark rose gallantly on the flood and began to move along. The unicorn swam alongside, and as it passed Og, the giant jumped on to its back.

"See, Father Noah," he cried, with a huge chuckle, "you will have to save me after all. I will snatch all the food you put through the window for the unicorn."

Noah saw that it was useless to argue with Og, who might, indeed, sink the Ark with his tremendous strength.

"I will make a bargain with you," he shouted from a window. "I will feed you, but you must promise to be a servant to my descendants."

Og was very hungry, so he accepted the conditions and devoured his first breakfast.

The rain continued to fall in great big sheets that shut out the light of day. Inside the Ark, however, all was bright and cheerful, for Noah had collected the most precious of the stones of the earth and had used them for the windows. Their radiance illumined the whole of the three stories in the Ark. Some of the animals were troublesome and Noah got no sleep at all. The lion had a bad attack of fever. In a corner a bird slept the whole of the time. This was the phoenix.

"Wake up," said Noah, one day. "It is feeding time."

"Thank you," returned the bird. "I saw you were busy, Father Noah, so I would not trouble you."

"You are a good bird," said Noah, much touched, "therefore you shall never die."

One day the rain ceased, the clouds rolled away and the sun shone brilliantly again. How strange the world looked! It was like a vast ocean. Nothing but water could be seen anywhere, and only one or two of the highest mountain tops peeped above the flood. All the world was drowned, and Noah gazed on the desolate scene from one of the windows with tears in his eyes. Og, riding gaily on the unicorn behind the Ark, was quite happy.

"Ha, ha!" he laughed gleefully. "I shall be able to eat and drink just as much as I like now and shall never be troubled by those tiny little creatures, the mortals."

"Don't be so sure," said Noah. "Those tiny mortals shall be your masters, and shall outlive you and the whole race of giants and demons."

The giant did not relish this prospect. He knew that whatever Noah prophesied would come true, and he was so sad that he ate no food for two days and began to grow smaller and thinner. He became more and more unhappy as day by day the water subsided and the mountains began to appear. At last the Ark rested on Mount Ararat, and Og's long ride came to an end.

"I will soon leave you, Father Noah," he said. "I shall wander round the world to see what is left of it."

"You cannot go until I permit you," said Noah. "Have you forgotten our compact so soon? You must be my servant. I have work for you."

Giants are not fond of work, and Og, who was the father of all the giants, was particularly lazy. He cared only to eat and sleep, but he knew he was in Noah's power, and he shed bitter tears when he saw the land appear again.

"Stop," commanded Noah. "Do you wish to drown the world once more with your big tears?"

So, Og sat on a mountain and rocked from side to side, weeping silently to himself. He watched the animals leave the Ark, meaning that he had to do all the hard work when Noah's children went off to build houses. Daily he complained that he was shrinking to the size of the mortals, for Noah said there was not too much food.

One day Noah said to him, "Come with me, Og. I am going around the world. I am commanded to plant fruit and flowers to make the earth beautiful. I need your help."

For many days they wandered all over the earth, and Og was compelled to carry the heavy bag of seeds. The last thing Noah planted was the grape vine.

"What is this, food, or drink?" asked Og.

"Both," replied Noah. "It can be eaten, or its juice made into wine," and as he planted it, he blessed the grape. "Be," he said, "a plant pleasing to the eye, bear fruit that will be food for the hungry and a health-giving drink to the thirsty and sick."

Og grunted. "I will offer up sacrifice to this wonderful fruit," he said. "May I not do so now that our labours are over?"

Noah agreed, and the giant brought a sheep, a lion, a pig and a monkey. First, he slaughtered the sheep, then the lion.

"When a man shall taste but a few drops of the wine," he said, "he shall be as harmless as a sheep. When he takes a little more he shall be as strong as a lion."

Then Og began to dance around the plant, and he killed the pig and the monkey. Noah was very much surprised.

"I am giving your descendants two extra blessings," said Og, chuckling. He rolled over and over on the ground in great glee and then said, "When a man shall drink too much of the juice of the wine, then shall he become a beast like the pig, and if then he still continues to drink, he shall behave foolishly like a monkey."

And that is why, to this day, too much wine makes a man silly.

Og himself often drank too much, and many years afterward, when he was a servant to the patriarch Abraham, the latter scolded him until he became so frightened that he dropped a tooth. Abraham made an ivory chair for himself from this tooth. Afterwards Og became King of Bashan, but he forgot his compact with Noah and instead of helping the Israelites to obtain Canaan he opposed them.

"I will kill them all with one blow," he declared.

Exerting all his enormous strength he uprooted a mountain and raising it high above his head he prepared to drop it on the camp of the Israelites and crush it.

But a wonderful thing happened. The mountain was full of grasshoppers and ants who had bored millions of tiny holes in it. When King Og raised the great mass, it crumbled in his hands and fell over his head and round his neck like a collar. He tried to pull it off, but his teeth became entangled in the mass. As he danced about in rage and pain, Moses, the leader of the Israelites, approached him.

Moses was a tiny man compared with Og. He was only ten ells high, and he carried with him a sword of the same length. With a mighty effort he jumped ten ells into the air, and raising the sword, he managed to strike the giant on the ankle and wound him mortally.

Thus, after many years, did the terrible giant of the flood perish for breaking his word to Father Noah.

Alexander's Conquests

This story has been adapted from James Johonnot's version of the same tale that originally appeared in Stories of the Olden Time, published in 1889 by D. Appleton and Company. This tale is based on earlier work undertaken by Charlotte M. Yonge.

In moving his army to the East, Alexander crossed the Euphrates and Tigris without opposition, and the decisive battle did not take place till he reached the plain of Arbela, where the Persians were drawn up to receive him. The Macedonians wished to make a night attack, but Alexander would not permit it, saying that he disdained to steal a victory, and the combat took place the next day.

The army of Persians was drawn from the more remote regions of Bactria and Parthia, where the men were more warlike, and they fought better than any whom the Macedonians had before encountered, but Darius himself fled early in the day, leaving behind him his bow and shield. His men lost courage, and followed him, and Alexander was left master of the field of Arbela.

This battle placed in his power all the western part of the Persian empire, and he had only to march to the great cities of Babylon, Susa, Ecbatana, and Persepolis, to take possession of the huge stores of treasures heaped up there by the Persian kings, which he now distributed among his followers with royal bounty. The unfortunate

Darius escaped into Bactria, where two satraps, in whom he had confided, treacherously seized him and made him prisoner, carrying him along with them as they fled before Alexander, until at length, being closely pressed by the Greeks, they threw their darts at him, and left him lying on the ground mortally wounded.

Darius was still alive when some of the Greeks came up, but died before the arrival of Alexander. The conqueror wept as he beheld the corpse of the last of a line of such great princes. He threw his own cloak over the body, and sent it to Babylon, where it was buried with great magnificence.

The wife of Darius had died a prisoner, but Sisygambis, his mother, still remained with her grandchildren at Babylon. Only once does Alexander seem to have hurt her feelings, and this was through ignorance of Persian customs. He showed her some robes of his sister's own weaving and embroidery and offered to have her granddaughters instructed in the same art, at which she wept, since Persian ladies deemed such employment work fit only for slaves and captives, and Alexander was obliged to explain how honourably the loom and needle were esteemed by his own countrywomen.

Alexander was much attached to his own mother, Olympias, and portions of his letters to her have come down to our time. She was a proud and violent woman, who often interfered with Antipater, governor of Macedon, and caused him to send many complaints to the king.

"Ah!" said Alexander, "Antipater does not know that one tear of a mother will blot out ten thousand of his letters."

Alexander had indeed an open and affectionate heart, but he was fast becoming too much uplifted by his successes. On Darius's death, he took the state as well as the title of a king of Persia, wore the tiara and robes, and claimed from the Macedonians the same servile tokens of homage as were paid by the eastern nations, thus causing perpetual heart-burnings among them, since they could neither endure to see their king exalted so much further above them, nor to be placed on the same level with the barbarians whom they despised.

Their jealousies troubled Alexander from the time he assumed the tiara of Persia. He found it impossible to raise the condition of the Persians, and treat them with favour, without offending the Macedonians, and his temper did not always endure these provocations. The worst action of his life was the sentencing to death, on a false accusation, the wise old General Parmenio, and his son, and in a fit of passion at a riotous banquet, he slew, with his own hand, his friend Clitus, his nurse's son, who had saved his life at the battle of Granicus. It was the deed of a moment of drunken violence, and he bitterly lamented it, shutting himself up for several days without allowing any one to approach him, and paying all honours to the memory of his murdered friend.

His pride and vain-glory went so far, that he declared that the oracle of Jupiter Ammon had announced that he was the son of Jupiter, and sent word back to Greece stating his desire to be enrolled among the gods in his life-time. Some of the Greeks were shocked at his profanity, others laughed at him, but all the Spartans said was, "If Alexander will be a god, let him."

The next four years were the most laborious of Alexander's life. He pursued the murderers of Darius into Bactria and Sogdiana, avenged his death, and reduced the numerous hill-forts as far as the frontier of Scythia. Fierce insurrections broke out among the wild tribes of Sogdiana, which it required all his activity and judgment to quell, and more than once provoked him into cruelty, though in general, conqueror as he was, he was no spoiler, but wherever he went founded cities, and tried to teach the Persians the civilized arts of Greece.

In 326 he set out for India, as the region was called round the river Indus. Here the inhabitants were warlike, and Porus, king of a portion of the country, made a brave resistance, but was at length defeated and taken prisoner. On being brought before Alexander he said he had nothing to ask, save to be treated as a king. "That I shall do for my own sake," said Alexander, and accordingly not only set him at liberty, but enlarged his territory.

All these Indian nations brought a tribute of elephants, which the Macedonians now for the first time learned to employ in war. Alexander wished to proceed into Hindostan, a country hitherto entirely unknown, but his soldiers grew so discontented at the prospect of being led so much farther from home, into the utmost parts of the earth, that he was obliged to give up his attempt, and very unwillingly turned back from the banks of the Sutlej.

While returning, he besieged a little town belonging to a tribe called the Malli, and believed to be the present city of Multan. He was the first to scale the wall, and after four others had mounted, the ladder broke, and he was left standing on the wall, a mark for the darts of the enemy. He instantly leaped down within the wall into the midst of the Malli, and there setting his back against a fig-tree, defended himself until a barbed arrow deeply pierced his breast, and, after trying to keep up a little longer, he sunk, fainting, on his shield. His four companions sprung down after him. Two were slain, but the others held their shields over him till the rest of the army succeeded in breaking into the town and coming to the rescue.

14. His wound was severe and dangerous, but he at length recovered, sailed down to the mouth of the Indus, and sent a fleet to survey the

Persian Gulf, while he himself marched along the shore. The country was bare and desert, and his army suffered dreadfully from heat, thirst, and hunger, while he readily shared all their privations. A little water was once brought him on a parching day, as a great prize, but since there was not enough for all, he poured it out on the sand, lest his faithful followers should feel themselves thirstier when they saw him drink alone.

At last he safely arrived at Caramania, where he returned to the more inhabited and wealthy parts of Persia, held his court with great magnificence at Susa, and then went to Babylon. Here embassies met him from every part of the known world, bringing gifts and homage, and above all, there arrived from the Greek states the much desired promise that he should be honoured as a god. He was at the highest pitch of worldly greatness to which mortal man had yet attained, and his designs were reaching yet further, but his hour was come, and at Babylon, the home of pride, "the great horn" was to be broken.

In the marshes into which the Euphrates had spread since its channel was altered by Cyrus, there breathed a noxious air, and a few weeks after Alexander's arrival, he was attacked by a fever, perhaps increased by intemperance. He bore up against it as long as possible, continued to offer sacrifices daily, though with increasing difficulty, and summoned his officers to arrange plans for his intended expedition. His strength failed him on the ninth day, and though he called them together as usual, he could not address them. Perhaps he thought in that hour of the prophecy he had seen at Jerusalem, that the empire he had toiled to raise should be divided, for he is reported to have said that there would be a mighty contest at his funeral games. He made no attempt to name a successor, but he took off his signet-ring, placed it on the finger of Perdiccas, one of his generals, and a short time after expired, in the thirty-third year of his age, and the twelfth of his reign.

There was a voice of wailing throughout the city that night. The Babylonians shut up their houses, and trembled at the neighbourhood of the fierce Greek soldiery now that their protector was dead. The Macedonians stood to arms all night, as if in presence of the enemy, and when in the morning the officers assembled in the palace council chamber, bitter and irrepressible was the burst of lamentation that broke out at the sight of the vacant throne, where lay the crown, sceptre, and royal robes, and where Perdiccas now placed the signet-ring. More deeply than all mourned the prisoner, the aged Sisygambis, who covered her face with a black veil, sat down in a corner of her room, refused all entreaties to speak or to eat, and expired five days after Alexander.

Nor did the Persians soon cease to lament the conqueror, who had ruled them more beneficently than their own monarchs had done. Their traditions made Alexander a prince of their own, and adorned him with every virtue valued in the East. That he had many great faults has already been shown, and, of course, by the rules of justice, his conquests were but reckless gratifications of his own ambition, but he was a high-minded, generous man, open of heart, free of hand, and for the most part acting up to his knowledge of right, and if unbridled power, talent of the highest order, and glory such as none before or since has ever attained, inflamed his passions, and elated him with pride, still it is not for us to judge severely of one who had such great temptations, and so little to guide him aright.

The Bride Of The Fountain

This story has been adapted from Abraham G. Seklemian's version of the same tale that originally appeared in The Golden Maiden and Other Folk Tales and Fairy Stories Told in Armenia, published in 1898 by The Helman-Taylor Company, New York. This tale is based on earlier work undertaken by Ohannes Chatschumian, who, before his death, had begun a compilation of 'Armenian' folklore for Miss Alice Fletcher. These 'Armenian' tales themselves originated in the Byzantine peasant tradition that developed over the preceding fifteen hundred years.

There were once three sisters, whose mother went to town to buy them dresses. On her way back to the village she sat down by a fountain to rest.

"Tush!" she exclaimed, remembering that she had forgotten to buy a dress for her youngest daughter.

Suddenly an old man came out from the fountain, and standing before the woman, said, "My name is Tush. Why did you call me?"

"I did not call you," said the woman. "I exclaimed, 'Tush!' because I had forgotten to buy a dress for my youngest daughter."

"Go, bring her," said the old man, "and call on me again, for I will give her a dress."

The woman went and brought her daughter to the fountain. As soon as she uttered the word "Tush!" the old man came out. He took the maiden into the fountain and never came back, in spite of the repeated exclamations of the woman, who eventually tired of repeating, "Tush! Tush!" At last she gave up hope, and going home mourned the wonderful disappearance of her pretty daughter. After one or two months she went again to the fountain and uttered the word "Tush!" The old man came out, and seeing the woman he turned toward the fountain, saying, "Hello! Son, your mother-in-law has come to call on her daughter. Won't you send her out?"

"Certainly," said a voice from within. "I will send her to pay a visit to her mother, as is the custom."

In a few minutes the anxious mother saw her daughter come out from the fountain dressed as a beautiful bride, and she took her home.

"Mamma," said the bride, "give me a separate room. My husband told me that he will come to me every night."

The mother gave her a separate room. The bridegroom visited her every night in the shape of a partridge. He used to come after nightfall, and flapping his wings, perch on the window ledge. She opened the window and took him in. Every morning the partridge flew away before dawn. Her two sisters, envious of the happiness of their youngest sister, brought razors and nailed them around the window. At nightfall the partridge came flying, and when he was perching on the window he struck his wings against the razors, which wounded his body in several places. He was hardly able to fly back to his fountain, and there he was confined to his bed. He vowed to be revenged upon his bride, who he thought had put the razors on the window. The bride, seeing that the partridge did not come for five or six days, went with her mother to the fountain.

"Tush!" they called, and the old man came out, and turning to the fountain, exclaimed, "Son, your bride and mother-in-law have come."

"Oh, oh!" cried the partridge from within, "I do not want such a bride. I beseech you, put on your eagle's suit, take her to the seventh heaven, and there cast her to the torrid desert."

Father Tush at once changed himself into an eagle, and carried the bride away and cast her to the sandy desert. There she fell upon the sand, but did not die.

"O Heaven!" exclaimed the maiden, "What have I done to deserve such treatment."

She wandered about in the desert without knowing where to go. At nightfall she buried herself in the sand to sleep. Soon two conjurers came along, who sat down near her. They conjured, and innumerable great serpents gathered around them. They sat in council, inquired of each other, and prepared remedies for a thousand and one diseases. For razor cuts they devised this remedy, "Wash the patient with the first milk from the breasts of a woman, and put upon the wounds the dried blood taken from a young woman's veins. On the third application the patient will be healed."

The maiden, who was listening to them attentively, kept that remedy in mind, and on the following morning started for her husband's fountain. After a long journey, she came to her own country, begged from the village women a mother's first milk, and opening one of her own veins, got some blood which she dried in the sun. She then went to the fountain disguised as a lad.

"Tush!" she exclaimed, and the old man came out.

"What do you want?" said he.

"I am a doctor," she said. "I had forgotten to get some of my medicines in the village, therefore I said 'Tush!'"

The old man went in and informed his son that there was a human doctor at the fountain.

"Bring him in," said the lad, "let us see if he can administer some remedy to my wounds."

The maiden went in, and after an examination said, "I can heal you within three days."

She washed him with the milk and put the dried blood on the wounds, and on the third day the lad was healed.

"What do you want me to pay you?" said the lad.

"I do not want anything," said the maiden, "I wish you only to remember my name."

"What is it?" asked the lad.

"Incense-Tree is my name," answered the maiden.

"Ah," exclaimed the lad, "that is my wife's name!"

"I am your wife," said she, throwing away her masculine attire.

She fell on his neck sobbing, and told him how without a fault she was. They loved each other thereafter, and are still living in that deep fountain.

The Fairy Princess Of Ergetz

This story has been adapted from Gertrude Landa's version of the same tale that originally appeared in Jewish Fairy Tales and Legends, published in 1943 by Bloch Publishing Co. Inc., New York.

I

In a great and beautiful city that stood by the sea, an old man lay dying. Mar Shalmon was his name, and he was the richest man in the land. Propped up with pillows on a richly decorated bed in a luxurious chamber, he gazed, with tears in his eyes, through the open window at the setting sun. Like a ball of fire it sank lower and lower until it almost seemed to rest on the tranquil waters beyond the harbour. Suddenly, Mar Shalmon roused himself.

"Where is my son, Bar Shalmon?" he asked in a feeble voice, and his hand crept tremblingly along the silken coverlet of the bed as if in search of something.

"I am here, my father," replied his son who was standing by the side of his bed. His eyes were moist with tears, but his voice was steady.

"My son," said the old man, slowly, and with some difficulty, "I am about to leave this world. My soul will take flight from this frail body when the sun has sunk behind the horizon. I have lived long and have amassed great wealth which will soon be yours. Use it well, as I have taught you, for you, my son, are a man of learning, as befits our noble Jewish faith. One thing I must ask you to promise me."

"I will, my father," returned Bar Shalmon, sobbing.

"No, do not weep, my son," said the old man. "My day is ended, but my life has not been ill-spent. I would spare you the pain that was mine in my early days, when, as a merchant, I garnered my fortune. The sea out there is calm now and will soon swallow up the sun. But beware of it, my son, for it is treacherous. Promise me… no, swear to me that you will never cross it to foreign lands."

Bar Shalmon placed his hands on those of his father. "Solemnly I swear," he said, in a broken voice, "to do your wish. I will never journey on the sea, but will remain here in this, my native land. 'Tis a vow before you, my father."

"'Tis an oath before heaven," said the old man. "Guard it, keep it, and heaven will bless you. Remember! See, the sun is sinking."

Mar Shalmon fell back upon his pillows and spoke no more. Bar Shalmon stood gazing out of the window until the sun had disappeared, and then, silently sobbing, he left the chamber of death.

The whole city wept when the sad news was made known, for Mar Shalmon was a man of great charity, and almost all the inhabitants followed the remains to the grave. Then Bar Shalmon, his son, took his father's place of honour in the city, and in him, too, the poor and needy found a friend whose purse was ever open and whose counsel was ever wisdom.

Thus years passed away.

One day there arrived in the harbour of the city a strange ship from a distant land. Its captain spoke a tongue unknown, and Bar Shalmon, being a man of profound knowledge, was sent for. He alone in the city could understand the language of the captain. To his astonishment, he learned that the cargo of the vessel was for Mar Shalmon, his father.

"I am the son of Mar Shalmon," he said. "My father is dead, and all his possessions he left to me."

"Then, truly, are you the most fortunate mortal, and the richest, on earth," answered the captain. "My good ship is filled with a vast store of jewels, precious stones and other treasures. And understand, oh most favoured son of Mar Shalmon, this cargo is but a small portion of the wealth that is yours in a land across the sea."

"'Tis strange," said Bar Shalmon, in surprise. "My father said nothing of this to me. I knew that in his younger days he had traded with distant lands, but he said nothing of possessions there. And, moreover, he warned me never to leave this shore."

The captain looked perplexed. "I don't understand it," the captain said. "I am only performing my father's bidding. He was your father's servant, and long years did he wait for Mar Shalmon's return to claim his riches. On his death-bed he bade me vow that I would seek his master, or his son, and this have I done."

He produced documents, and there could be no doubt that the vast wealth mentioned in them belonged now to Bar Shalmon.

"You are now my master," said the captain, "and must return with me to the land across the sea to claim your inheritance. In another year it will be too late, for by the laws of the country it will be forfeit."

"I cannot return with you," said Bar Shalmon. "I have a vow before heaven never to voyage on the sea."

The captain laughed. "In very truth, I do not understand you, just as my father did not understand your own father," he replied. "My father was wont to say that Mar Shalmon was strange and peradventure not possessed of all his senses to neglect his store of wealth and treasure."

With an angry gesture Bar Shalmon stopped the captain, but he was sorely troubled. He recalled now that his father had often spoken mysteriously of foreign lands, and he wondered, indeed, whether Mar Shalmon could have been in his proper senses not to have breathed a word of his riches abroad. For days he discussed the matter with the captain, who at last persuaded him to make the journey.

"Fear not your vow," said the captain. "Your worthy father must, of a truth, have been bereft of reason in failing to tell you of his full estate, and an oath to a man of unsound mind is not binding. That is the law in our land."

"So it is here," returned Bar Shalmon, and with this remark his last scruple vanished.

He bade a tender farewell to his wife, his child, and his friends, and set sail on the strange ship to the land beyond the sea.

For three days all went well, but on the fourth the ship was becalmed and the sails flapped lazily against the masts. The sailors had nothing to do but lie on deck and wait for a breeze, and Bar Shalmon took advantage of the occasion to treat them to a feast.

Suddenly, in the midst of the feasting, they felt the ship begin to move. There was no wind, but the vessel sped along very swiftly. The captain himself rushed to the helm. To his alarm he found the vessel beyond control.

"The ship is bewitched," he exclaimed. "There is no wind, and no current, and yet we are being borne along as if driven before a storm. We shall be lost."

Panic seized the sailors, and Bar Shalmon was unable to pacify them.

"Someone on board has brought us ill-luck," said the boatswain, looking pointedly at Bar Shalmon, "we shall have to heave him overboard."

His comrades assented and rushed toward Bar Shalmon.

Just at that moment, however, the look-out in the bow cried excitedly, "Land ahead!"

The ship still refused to answer the helm and grounded on a sandbank. She shivered from stem to stern but did not break up. No rocks were visible, only a desolate tract of desert land was to be seen, with here and there a solitary tree.

"We seem to have sustained no damage," said the captain, when he had recovered from his first astonishment, "but how we are going to get afloat again I do not know. This land is quite strange to me."

He could not find it marked on any of his charts or maps, and the sailors stood looking gloomily at the mysterious shore.

"Should we explore the land?" said Bar Shalmon.

"No, no," exclaimed the boatswain, excitedly. "See, no breakers strike on the shore. This is not a human land. This is a domain of demons. We are lost unless we cast overboard the one who has brought on us this ill-luck."

Said Bar Shalmon, "I will land, and I will give fifty silver crowns to all who land with me."

Not one of the sailors moved, however, even when he offered fifty golden crowns, and at last Bar Shalmon said he would land alone, although the captain strongly urged him not to do so.

Bar Shalmon sprang lightly to the shore, and as he did so the ship shook violently.

"What did I tell you?" shouted the boatswain. "Bar Shalmon is the one who has brought us this misfortune. Now we shall refloat the ship."

But it still remained firmly fixed on the sand. Bar Shalmon walked towards a tree and climbed it. In a few moments he returned, holding a twig in his hand.

"The land stretches away for miles just as you see it here," he called to the captain. "There is no sign of man or habitation."

He prepared to board the vessel again, but the sailors would not allow him. The boatswain stood in the bow and threatened him with a sword. Bar Shalmon raised the twig to ward off the blow and struck the ship which shivered from stern to stern again.

"Is this not proof that the vessel is bewitched?" cried the sailors, and when the captain sternly bade them remember that Bar Shalmon was their master, they threatened him too.

Bar Shalmon, amused at the fears of the men, again struck the vessel with the twig. Once more it trembled. A third time he raised the twig. "If the ship is bewitched," he said, "something will happen after the third blow."

"Swish" sounded the branch through the air, and the third blow fell on the vessel's bow. Something did happen. The ship almost leaped from the sand, and before Bar Shalmon could realize what had happened it was speeding swiftly away.

"Come back, come back," he screamed, and he could see the captain struggling with the helm. But the vessel refused to answer, and Bar Shalmon saw it grow smaller and smaller and finally disappear. He was alone on an uninhabited desert land.

"What a wretched plight for the richest man in the world," he said to himself, and the next moment he realized that he was in danger indeed.

A terrible roar made him look around. To his horror he saw a lion making toward him. As quick as a flash Bar Shalmon ran to the tree and hastily scrambled into the branches. The lion dashed itself furiously against the trunk of the tree, but, for the present, Bar Shalmon was safe. Night, however, was coming on, and the lion squatted at the foot of the tree, evidently intending to wait for him. All night the lion remained, roaring at intervals, and Bar Shalmon clung to one of the upper branches afraid to sleep lest he should fall off and be devoured. When morning broke, a new danger threatened him. A huge eagle flew round the tree and darted at him with its cruel beak. Then the great bird settled on the thickest branch, and Bar Shalmon moved stealthily forward with a knife which he drew from his belt. He crept behind the bird, but as he approached it spread its big wings, and Bar Shalmon, to prevent himself being swept from the tree, dropped the knife and clutched at the bird's feathers. Immediately, to his dismay, the bird rose from the tree. Bar Shalmon clung to its back with all his might.

Higher and higher soared the eagle until the trees below looked like mere dots on the land. The eagle flew swiftly over miles and miles of desert until Bar Shalmon began to feel giddy. He was faint with hunger and feared that he would not be able to retain his hold. All day the bird flew without resting, across island and sea. No houses, no ships, no human beings could be seen. Toward night, however,

Bar Shalmon, to his great joy, beheld the lights of a city surrounded by trees, and as the eagle came near, he made a bold dive to the earth. Headlong he plunged downward. He seemed to be hours in falling. At last he struck a tree, where the branches broke beneath the weight and force of his falling body, and he continued to plunge downward. The branches tore his clothes to shreds and bruised his body, but they broke his terrible fall, and when at last he reached the ground he was not much hurt.

II

Bar Shalmon found himself on the outskirts of the city, and he crept forward with care. To his intense relief, he saw that the first building was a synagogue. The door, however, was locked. Weary, sore, and weak with long fasting, Bar Shalmon sank down on the steps and sobbed like a child.

Something touched him on the arm. He looked up. By the light of the moon he saw a boy standing before him. Such a queer boy he was, too. He had cloven feet, and his coat, if it was a coat, seemed to be made in the shape of wings.

"*Ivri Onochi*," said Bar Shalmon, "I am a Hebrew."

"So am I," said the boy. "Follow me."

He walked in front with a strange hobble, and when they reached a house at the back of the synagogue, he leaped from the ground, spreading his coat wings as he did so, to a window about twenty feet from the ground. The next moment a door opened, and Bar Shalmon, to his surprise, saw that the boy had jumped straight through the window down to the door which he had unfastened from the inside. The boy motioned him to enter a room. He did so, and an aged man, who he saw was a rabbi, rose to greet him.

"Peace be with you," said the rabbi, and pointed to a seat. He clapped his hand and immediately a table with food appeared before Bar Shalmon. The latter was far too hungry to ask any questions just then, and the rabbi was silent, too, while he ate. When he had finished, the rabbi clapped his hands and the table vanished.

"Now tell me your story," said the rabbi.

Bar Shalmon did so. "Alas! I am an unhappy man," he concluded. "I have been punished for breaking my vow. Help me to return to my home. I will reward you well, and will atone for my sin."

"Your story is indeed sad," said the rabbi, gravely, "but you do not know the full extent of your unfortunate plight. Are you aware what land it is into which you have been cast?"

"No," said Bar Shalmon, becoming afraid again.

"Know then," said the rabbi. "You are not in a land of human beings. You have fallen into Ergetz, the land of demons, of djinns, and of fairies."

"But are you not a Jew?" asked Bar Shalmon, in astonishment.

"Truly," replied the rabbi. "Even in this realm we have all manner of religions just as you mortals have."

"What will happen to me?" asked Bar Shalmon, in a whisper.

"I don't know," replied the rabbi. "Few mortals come here, and mostly, I fear they are put to death. The demons do not love them."

"Woe, woe is me," cried Bar Shalmon, "I am undone."

"Do not weep," said the rabbi. "I, as a Jew, hate death by violence and torture, and will endeavour to save you."

"I thank you," cried Bar Shalmon.

"Let your thanks wait," said the rabbi, kindly. "There is human blood in my veins. My great-grandfather was a mortal who fell into this land and was not put to death. Being of mortal descent, I have been made rabbi. Perhaps you will find favour here and be permitted to live and settle in this land."

"But I desire to return home," said Bar Shalmon.

The rabbi shook his head. "You must sleep now," he said.

He passed his hands over Bar Shalmon's eyes and he fell into a profound slumber. When he awoke it was daylight, and the boy stood by his couch. He made a sign to Bar Shalmon to follow, and through an underground passage he conducted him into the synagogue and placed him near the rabbi.

"Your presence has become known," whispered the rabbi, and even as he spoke a great noise was heard. It was like the wild chattering of many high-pitched voices. Through all the windows and the doors a strange crowd poured into the synagogue. There were demons of all shapes and sizes. Some had big bodies with tiny heads, others huge heads and quaint little bodies. Some had great staring eyes, others had long wide mouths, and many had only one leg each. They surrounded Bar Shalmon with threatening gestures and noises. The rabbi ascended the pulpit.

"Silence!" he commanded, and immediately the noise ceased. "You who thirst for mortal blood, do not desecrate this holy building wherein I am master. What you have to say must wait until after the morning service."

Silently and patiently they waited, sitting in all manner of queer places. Some of them perched on the backs of the seats, a few clung like great big flies to the pillars, others sat on the window-sills, and several of the tiniest hung from the rafters in the ceiling. As soon as the service was over, the clamour broke out anew.

"Give us the perjurer," screamed the demons. "He is not fit to live."

With some difficulty, the rabbi stilled the tumult, and said, "Listen to me, you demons and sprites of the land of Ergetz. This man has fallen into my hands, and I am responsible for him. Our king, Ashmedai, must know of his arrival. We must not condemn a man unheard. Let us petition the king to grant him a fair trial."

After some demur, the demons agreed to this proposal, and they trooped out of the synagogue in the same peculiar manner in which they came. Each was compelled to leave by the same door or window at which he entered.

Bar Shalmon was carried off to the palace of King Ashmedai, preceded and followed by a noisy crowd of demons and fairies. There seemed to be millions of them, all clattering and pointing at him. They hobbled and hopped over the ground, jumped into the air, sprang from housetop to housetop, made sudden appearances from holes in the ground and vanished through solid walls.

The palace was a vast building of white marble that seemed as delicate as lace work. It stood in a magnificent square where many beautiful fountains spouted jets of crystal water. King Ashmedai came forth on the balcony, and at his appearance all the demons and fairies became silent and went down on their knees.

"What do want with me?" he cried, in a voice of thunder, and the rabbi approached and bowed before his majesty.

"A mortal, a Jew, has fallen into my hands," he said, "and your subjects crave his blood. He is a perjurer, they say. Gracious majesty, I would petition for a trial."

"What manner of mortal is he?" asked Ashmedai.

Bar Shalmon stepped forward.

"Jump up here so I may see you," commanded the king.

"Jump, jump," cried the crowd.

"I cannot," said Bar Shalmon, as he looked up at the balcony thirty feet above the ground.

"Try," said the rabbi.

Bar Shalmon did try, and found, the moment he lifted his feet from the ground, that he was standing on the balcony.

"Neatly done," said the king. "I see you are quick at learning."

"So my teachers always said," replied Bar Shalmon.

"A proper answer," said the king. "You are, then, a scholar?"

"In my own land," returned Bar Shalmon, "men said I was great among the learned."

"So," said the king. "And can you teach the wisdom of man and of the human world to others?"

"I can," said Bar Shalmon.

"We shall see," said the king. "I have a son with a desire for such knowledge. If you can make him acquainted with your store of learning, your life shall be spared. The petition for a trial is granted."

The king waved his sceptre and two slaves seized Bar Shalmon by the arms. He felt himself lifted from the balcony and carried swiftly through the air. Across the vast square the slaves flew with him, and when over the largest of the fountains they loosened their hold. Bar Shalmon thought he would fall into the fountain, but to his amazement he found himself standing on the roof of a building. By his side was the rabbi.

"Where are we?" asked Bar Shalmon. "I feel bewildered."

"We are at the Court of Justice, one hundred miles from the palace," replied the rabbi.

A door appeared before them. They stepped through, and found themselves in a beautiful hall. Three judges in red robes and purple wigs were seated on a platform, and an immense crowd filled the galleries in the same queer way as in the synagogue. Bar Shalmon was placed on a small platform in front of the judges. A tiny sprite, only about six inches high, stood on another small platform at his right hand and commenced to read from a scroll that seemed to have no ending. He read the whole account of Bar Shalmon's life. Not one little event was missing.

"The charge against Bar Shalmon, the mortal," the sprite concluded, "is that he has violated the solemn oath sworn at his father's death-bed."

Then the rabbi pleaded for him and declared that the oath was not binding because Bar Shalmon's father had not informed him of his treasures abroad and could not therefore have been in his right senses. Further, he added, Bar Shalmon was a scholar and the king desired him to teach his wisdom to the crown prince.

The chief justice rose to pronounce sentence.

"Bar Shalmon," he said, "rightly you should die for your broken oath. It is a grievous sin. But there is the doubt that your father may not have been in his right mind. Therefore, your life shall be spared."

Bar Shalmon expressed his thanks.

"When may I return to my home?" he asked.

"Never," replied the chief justice.

Bar Shalmon left the court, feeling very downhearted. He was safe now. The demons dared not molest him, but he longed to return to his home.

"How am I to get back to the palace?" he asked the rabbi. "Perhaps after I have imparted my learning to the crown prince, the king will allow me to return to my native land."

"That I cannot say. Come, fly with me," said the rabbi.

"Fly!"

"Yes. Look, you have wings."

Bar Shalmon noticed that he was now wearing a garment just like all the demons. When he spread his arms, he found he could fly, and he sailed swiftly through the air to the palace. With these wings, he thought, he would be able to fly home.

"Don't think that," said the rabbi, who seemed to be able to read his thoughts, "for your wings are useless beyond this land."

Bar Shalmon found that it would be best for him to carry out his instructions for the present, and he set himself diligently to teach the crown prince. The prince was an apt pupil, and the two became great friends. King Ashmedai was delighted and made Bar Shalmon one of his favourites.

One day the king said to him, "I am about to leave the city for a while to undertake a campaign against a rebellious tribe of demons thousands of miles away. I must take the crown prince with me. I leave you in charge of the palace."

The king gave him a huge bunch of keys.

"These," he said, "will admit you into all but one of the thousand rooms in the palace. For that one there is no key, and you must not enter it. Beware."

For several days Bar Shalmon amused himself by examining the hundreds of rooms in the vast palace until one day he came to the door for which he had no key. He forgot the king's warning and his promise to obey.

"Open this door for me," he said to his attendants, but they replied that they could not.

"You must," he said angrily, "burst it open."

"We do not know how to burst open a door," they said. "We are not mortal. If we were permitted to enter the room we should just walk through the walls."

Bar Shalmon could not do this, so he put his shoulder to the door and it yielded quite easily.

A strange sight met his gaze. A beautiful woman, the most beautiful he had ever seen, was seated on a throne of gold, surrounded by fairy attendants who vanished the moment he entered.

"Who are you?" asked Bar Shalmon, in great astonishment.

"The daughter of the king," replied the princess, "and your future wife."

"Indeed! How do you know that?" he asked.

"You have broken your promise to my father, the king, not to enter this room," she replied. "Therefore, you must die, unless…"

"Tell me quickly," interrupted Bar Shalmon, turning pale. "How can my life be saved?"

"You must ask my father for my hand," replied the princess. "Only by becoming my husband can you be saved."

"But I have a wife and child in my native land," said Bar Shalmon, sorely troubled.

"You have now forfeited your hopes of return," said the princess, slowly. "Once more have you broken a promise. It seems to come easy to you now."

Bar Shalmon had no wish to die, and he waited, in fear and trembling for the king's return. Immediately he heard of King Ashmedai's approach, he hastened to meet him and flung himself on the ground at his majesty's feet. "O King," he cried, "I have seen your daughter, the princess, and I desire to make her my wife."

"I cannot refuse," returned the king. "Such is our law, that he who first sees the princess must become her husband, or die. But, have a care, Bar Shalmon. You must swear to love and be faithful ever."

"I swear," said Bar Shalmon.

The wedding took place with much ceremony. The princess was attended by a thousand fairy bridesmaids, and the whole city was brilliantly decorated and illuminated until Bar Shalmon was almost blinded by the dazzling spectacle.

The rabbi performed the marriage ceremony, and Bar Shalmon had to swear an oath by word of mouth and in writing that he loved the princess and would never desert her. He was given a beautiful palace full of jewels as a dowry, and the wedding festivities lasted six months. All the fairies and demons invited them in turn. They had to attend banquets and parties and dances in grottoes and caves and in the depths of the fairy fountains in the square. Never before in Ergetz had there been such elaborate rejoicings.

III

Some years rolled by and still Bar Shalmon thought of his native land. One day the princess found him weeping quietly.

"Why are you sad, husband mine?" she asked. "Do you no longer love me, and am I not beautiful now?"

"No, it is not that," he said, but for a long time he refused to say more. At last he confessed that he had an intense longing to see his home again.

"But you are bound to me by an oath," said the princess.

"I know," replied Bar Shalmon, "and I shall not break it. Permit me to visit my home for a brief while, and I will return and prove myself more devoted to you than ever."

On these conditions, the princess agreed that he should take leave for a whole year. A big, black demon flew swiftly with him to his native city.

No sooner had Bar Shalmon placed his feet on the ground than he determined not to return to the land of Ergetz. "Tell your royal mistress," he said to the demon, "that I shall never return to her."

He tore his clothes to make himself look poor, but his wife was overjoyed to see him. She had mourned him as dead. He did not tell of his adventures, but merely said he had been ship-wrecked and had worked his way back as a poor sailor. He was delighted to be among human beings again, to hear his own language and to see solid buildings that did not appear and disappear just when they pleased, and as the days passed he began to think his adventures in fairyland were just a dream.

Meanwhile, the princess waited patiently until the year was ended. Then she sent the big, black demon to bring Bar Shalmon back.

Bar Shalmon met the messenger one night when walking alone in his garden.

"I have come to take you back," said the demon.

Bar Shalmon was startled. He had forgotten that the year was up. He felt that he was lost, but as the demon did not seize him by force, he saw that there was a possibility of escape.

"Return and tell your mistress I refuse," he said.

"I will take you by force," said the demon.

"You cannot," Bar Shalmon said, "for I am the son-in-law of the king."

The demon was helpless and returned to Ergetz alone.

King Ashmedai was very angry, but the princess counselled patience. "I will devise means to bring my husband back," she said. "I will send other messengers."

Thus it was that Bar Shalmon found a troupe of beautiful fairies in the garden the next evening. They tried their utmost to induce him to return with them, but he would not listen. Every day different messengers came; big, ugly demons who threatened, pretty fairies who tried to coax him, and troublesome sprites and goblins who only annoyed him. Bar Shalmon could not move without encountering messengers from the princess in all manner of queer places. Nobody else could see them, and often he was heard talking to invisible people. His friends began to regard him as strange in his behaviour.

King Ashmedai grew angrier every day, and he threatened to go for Bar Shalmon himself.

"No, I will go," said the princess. "It will be impossible for my husband to resist me."

She selected a large number of attendants, and the swift flight of the princess and her retinue through the air caused a violent storm to rage over the lands they crossed. Like a thick black cloud they swooped down on the land where Bar Shalmon dwelt, and their weird cries seemed like the wild shrieking of a mighty hurricane. Down they swept in a tremendous storm such as the city had never known. Then, as quickly as it came, the storm ceased, and the people who had fled into their houses, ventured forth again.

The little son of Bar Shalmon went out into the garden, but quickly rushed back into the house.

"Father, come and see," he cried. "The garden is full of strange creatures brought by the storm. All manner of creeping, crawling things have invaded the garden; lizards, toads, and myriads of insects. The trees, the shrubs, the paths are covered, and some shine in the twilight like tiny lanterns."

Bar Shalmon went out into the garden, but he did not see toads and lizards. What he beheld was a vast array of demons and goblins and sprites, and in a rose-bush the princess, his wife, shining like a star, surrounded by her attendant fairies. She stretched forth her arms to him.

"Husband mine," she pleaded, "I have come to implore you to return to the land of Ergetz with me. Sadly have I missed you. I have waited for your coming, and difficult it has been to appease my father's anger. Come, husband mine, return with me; a great welcome awaits you."

"I will not return," said Bar Shalmon.

"Kill him, kill him!" shrieked the demons, and they surrounded him, gesticulating fiercely.

"No, do not harm him," commanded the princess. "Think well, Bar Shalmon, before you answer again. The sun has set and night is upon us. Think well, until sunrise. Come to me, return, and all shall be well. Refuse, and you shalt be dealt with as you have merited. Think well before the sunrise."

"And what will happen at sunrise, if I refuse?" asked Bar Shalmon.

"You shall see," returned the princess. "Think carefully, and remember, I will await you here until the sunrise."

"I have answered. I defy you," said Bar Shalmon, and he went indoors.

Night passed with strange, mournful music in the garden, and the sun rose in its glory and spread its golden beams over the city. And with the coming of the light, more strange sounds woke the people of the city. A wondrous sight met their gaze in the marketplace. It was filled with hundreds upon hundreds of the queerest creatures they had ever seen, goblins and brownies, demons and fairies. Dainty little elves ran about the square to the delight of the children, and quaint sprites clambered up the lampposts and squatted on the gables of the council house. On the steps of that building was a glittering array of fairies and attendant genii, and in their midst stood the princess, a dazzling vision, radiant as the dawn.

The mayor of the city did not know what to do. He put on his chain of office and made a long speech of welcome to the princess.

"Thank you for your cordial welcome," said the princess, in reply, "and you the mayor, and you the good people of this city of mortals, listen to me. I am the princess of the Fairyland of Ergetz where my father, Ashmedai, rules as king. There is one among you who is my husband."

"Who is he?" the crowd asked in astonishment.

"Bar Shalmon is his name," replied the princess, "and to him am I bound by vows that may not be broken."

"'Tis false," cried Bar Shalmon from the crowd.

"'Tis true. Behold our son," answered the princess, and there stepped forward a dainty elfin boy whose face was the image of Bar Shalmon.

"I ask of you mortals of the city," the princess continued, "but one thing, and that is justice, that same justice which we in the land of Ergetz gave to Bar Shalmon when, after breaking his oath to his father, he set sail for a foreign land and was delivered into our hands. We spared his life. We granted his petition for a new trial. I only ask that you should grant me the same petition. Hear me in your Court of Justice."

"Your request is reasonable, princess," said the mayor. "It shall not be said that strangers here are refused justice. Bar Shalmon, follow me."

He led the way into the Chamber of Justice, and the magistrates of the city heard all that the princess and her witnesses, among whom was the rabbi, had to say. They then listened to all that Bar Shalmon, had to say.

"'Tis plain," said the mayor, delivering judgment, "that her royal highness, the princess of the Fairyland of Ergetz, has spoken the truth. But in this city Bar Shalmon a wife and child to whom he is bound by ties that may not be broken. Bar Shalmon must divorce the princess and return to her the dowry received by him on their marriage."

"If such be your law, I am content," said the princess.

"What do you say, Bar Shalmon?" asked the mayor.

"Oh! I'm content," he answered gruffly. "I agree to anything that will rid me of the demon princess."

The princess flushed crimson with shame and rage at these cruel words.

"I do not deserve these cruel words," she exclaimed, proudly. "I have loved you, and have been faithful to you, Bar Shalmon. I accept the decree of your laws and shall return to the land of Ergetz a widow. I do not ask for your pity. I ask only for that which is my right, one last kiss."

"Very well," said Bar Shalmon, still more gruffly, "anything to have done with you."

The princess stepped proudly forward to him and kissed him on the lips. Bar Shalmon turned deadly pale and would have fallen had his friends not caught him.

"Take your punishment for all your sins," cried the princess, haughtily, "for your broken vows and your false promises, for your perjury to your God, to your father, to my father and to me."

As she spoke Bar Shalmon fell dead at her feet. At a sign from the princess, her retinue of fairies and demons flew out of the building and up into the air with their royal mistress in their midst and vanished.

The Legend Of Haic

This story has been adapted from Louis A. Boettiger's version of the same tale that originally appeared in Armenian Legends and Festivals, published in 1920 by University of Minnesota, Minneapolis.

Armenians do not call themselves Armenians nor their country Armenia. They are descendants of Haic, as the legend goes, who was the son of Togarmah, the son of Japhet, who was the son of Noah, and they call their country Haiasdan after the patriarchal progenitor of their people. Haic dwelt in the plain of Shinar and was a prefect or director in the building of the tower of Babel. He was as beautiful as a god and as strong as a giant, mighty in battle and especially adept in spear throwing. In the days of his youth, Bel or Nimrod, who was the patron god of Babylon, established himself over all and wished to be worshipped. But Haic refused to obey, and taking his sons, who numbered about three hundred, his daughters, his sheep and cattle, he journeyed north until he came to the land of Ararat. Bel tried in vain to persuade his rival to come back.

"You have departed and have settled in a chill and frosty region," urged the Assyrian god. "Soften your hard pride, change your coldness to geniality, be my subject and come and live a life of ease in my domain."

But Haic refused the cordial invitation, which so much angered Bel that the latter brought his army to force the Armenian hero into submission. Haic, however, was victorious, for he slew Bel with an arrow from his own bow. The place where Bel was buried is called "Kerezman," meaning grave, and is pointed out to this day. Armenians sing songs and tell stories of the great beauty and valour of Haic. He died at the age of four hundred in about 2028 B.C.

This oldest of Armenian legends, quaint and simple as it is in accounting for the beginnings of a people, savours of the Old Testament and is suggestive of the Assyrian invasion which took place about the ninth century before Christ. It is significant that the Armenians refused the protection of Bel, and that in the very beginning of their legendary history, they insisted on standing firm and maintaining their independence, for no single quality is more characteristic of this people than a proud, haughty, even at times disdainful independence. It is also suggestive that their patriarchal hero was no saint, but a mighty giant, as beautiful as he was strong, whose greatest pride was in the throwing of a spear, for his descendants have not been a peaceful people. To be sure, they were the first nation to be converted to Christianity, which would say little for their firmness and independence, were it not that the priest with the cross was followed by a powerful king with a sword at the head of an army that had learned to fight as the Romans fought. The songs that were sung in memory and honour of Haic are seldom sung today unless it be in some remote village.

Dyjhicon: The Coward-Hero

This story has been adapted from Abraham G. Seklemian's version of the same tale that originally appeared in The Golden Maiden and Other Folk Tales and Fairy Stories Told in Armenia, published in 1898 by The Helman-Taylor Company, New York. This tale is based on earlier work undertaken by Ohannes Chatschumian, who, before his death, had begun a compilation of 'Armenian' folklore for Miss Alice Fletcher. These 'Armenian' tales themselves originated in the Byzantine peasant tradition that developed over the preceding fifteen hundred years.

Dyjhicon was a poor unfortunate fellow who had only two goats and a cow. His wife was an ambitious woman, and annoyed him by her frequent demands.

"I want you to go out and work," she often said. "I want you to build a new house, I want to buy myself some new dresses, oxen and sheep, a horse and wagon."

Dyjhicon, tiring of her endless complaints and scoldings, one day took his great stick and drove his one cow out of the house, saying to himself, "Let me run from this wicked wife to the wilderness and there die."

This, of course, was exactly what the woman wanted. So, he ran from her and wandered in the wilderness. When he was hungry he milked the cow and drank the milk, and when he was tired he mounted the cow. He was very timid, a typical coward. The sight of a running rat was enough to make him tremble.

"Ah!" he thought, nevertheless. "It is better to be torn by wild beasts than to become the slave of a wicked woman."

One day, as the cow was pasturing on a green meadow and Dyjhicon was lying down lazily, the flies stung him. He cursed his wife and clapped his hands to kill the flies. Then he counted to see how many flies he had killed at one stroke, and they were seven in number. This encouraged him, and he took his knife and carved upon his stick these words:

"I am Dyjhicon. I have killed seven by one stroke of the hand."

Then he got astride the cow and rode away. After a long journey he came to a green meadow in the centre of which there was a magnificent castle with an orchard around it. He let the cow graze in the meadow and he lay down to sleep. Seven brothers lived in that castle. One of them, seeing Dyjhicon and his cow in the meadow came to find who it was that had ventured to enter their ground. Dyjhicon was sleeping, with his stick standing near him. The man approached and, reading the inscription, was terrified.

"What a hero!" he thought to himself, "He has killed seven men by one stroke of the hand. He must be a brave man, else he would not dare to sleep here so carelessly. What courage! What boldness! He has come so far without arms, without a horse, without a companion. This man is surely a great hero."

He went and informed his brothers as to what he had seen; and all the seven brothers came to pay their respects to the unknown hero, and to invite him to their humble home. The cow, being frightened by their approach, began to leap and bellow. Her voice wakened Dyjhicon, who, seeing seven men standing before him, was terrified, and snatching his club, stood aside trembling. The seven brothers thought that he was angry with them, and was trembling on account of his wrath, and that he would kill all of them by one stroke of his stick. Thereupon they began to supplicate him to pardon their rudeness in disturbing his repose. Then they invited him to go with them, saying, "We are seven brothers and have a great reputation as good fighters in this district. But we shall be entirely invincible if you will join us and become our elder brother. We will take great pleasure in placing our house and all that belongs to us at the service of such a hero as yourself."

Hearing this, Dyjhicon ceased trembling, and said, "Very well, let it be as you say."

They took him to the castle with great pomp and served to him a grand banquet, at which all the seven brothers stood before him, folding their arms upon their breasts and awaiting his permission to sit. Dyjhicon was in great alarm, his heart was faint and he had fallen into meditation as to the manner in which he might free himself from this perplexing situation. The seven brothers thought that he was not only a very brave hero, but was also such a great sage, that he did not care even to look at their faces. They began to cough in a low voice to draw his attention. On account of his internal fear Dyjhicon suddenly shook his head, and the seven brothers took this as a permission to sit.

After the banquet they said to him, "My lord, where have you left your horse, arms and servants? Will you command us to go and bring them?"

"Horse and arms are necessary for timid men," said Dyjhicon, "I have never had need of them. I use horse and arms only when I fight a great battle. As to servants, I never need them. All men are my servants. You see, I have come so far having only a cow and my stick. Dyjhicon is my name. I have killed seven by one stroke of the hand."

Their esteem and admiration for Dyjhicon increased every day, and at last they were so much fascinated by his alleged bravery that they gave him in marriage their only sister, who was a very beautiful maiden. Dyjhicon knew that he was unworthy, but he could not refuse this gift.

"Ah!" he said, "I will do you the favour of marrying her since you entreat me so earnestly."

They brought costly garments, and putting them on Dyjhicon, made him a handsome bridegroom. They had a splendid wedding festival which was reported in all neighboring countries. The four princes of the neighboring countries had asked the hand of the maiden in marriage, and all of them had been refused. Now hearing that the maiden was given in marriage to a stranger, the four princes waged war against the seven brothers. Dyjhicon, hearing this, was stricken with fear, and longed that the earth might open its mouth and swallow him. He thought to run away, but there were no means of escaping.

While he indulged in these sad meditations, the seven brothers came, and bowing down before him, said, "What is your order, my lord? Will you go fight yourself, or will you have us go first?"

This caused Dyjhicon's heart to melt. He began to tremble in his whole body, and to strike his teeth one against another. The seven brothers thought that it was because of his violent rage, and that in his fury he would destroy whole armies.

"My lord," they said, finally, "let us seven brothers go fight them at first, and if we find them hard to conquer we will send you word, that you may come to our assistance."

"Well, well, do so," answered Dyjhicon, somewhat relieved.

They went and began the battle. Their neighboring peoples were in constant terror of the seven brothers, who were famous as brave fighters. Now that they had also a brother-in-law who could kill seven men by one stroke of the hand, their foes were the more afraid of them. But this time the men of the four princes were united, and they fought with unusual zeal and determination. This caused the seven brothers to retreat a little, and they sent to brother Dyjhicon, saying, "We are in trouble. Come to our assistance."

A fast horse and magnificent arms awaited him. He began to curse the day when he came to that house. But what could he do now? At last he decided to go to the battle-field, cast himself against the swords of the enemy and die. Death was preferable to such a disgraceful life. As soon as he mounted the horse, the beast who knew that the rider was inexperienced, ran away like a winged eagle. Dyjhicon could not stop or manage it. The seven brothers thought he was so brave that he left the horse free in order to reach and slaughter the enemy. The horse broke into the line of the enemy, who began to fly, saying, "Who can stand before this great hero?"

In their hurry to retreat they began to slaughter one another. Dyjhicon, who had never been on horseback before, was so much afraid that he thought he was already lost. As the horse was running through the forest, he threw his arms around an oak tree and embraced it, letting the horse go from under him. The tree happened to be rotten and was rooted out when he took hold of it. This caused a great panic among the enemy, who ran away exclaiming, "Aha! He has pulled up an enormous oak by the roots, and now he means to batter us into pieces with it. Who can stand before this strong warrior?"

So crying as they ran away, they slaughtered one another. Thereupon, the seven brothers came and embracing the feet of their heroic brother-in-law, exclaimed, "What magnificent courage! What a great victory!"

With these words they brought Dyjhicon home with great pomp and glory. The four princes who waged the war, being greatly humiliated, sued for reconciliation, and in order to gain Dyjhicon's favour, each of them sent him as a present one thousand ewes with their lambs, ten mares with their colts, and other costly offerings.

Thus the greatest coward became the greatest hero.

The Princess Of The Tower

This story has been adapted from Gertrude Landa's version of the same tale that originally appeared in Jewish Fairy Tales and Legends, published in 1943 by Bloch Publishing Co. Inc., New York.

I

Princess Solima was sick, not exactly ill, but so much out of sorts that her father, King Zuliman, was both annoyed and perturbed. The princess was as beautiful as a princess of those days should be. Her long tresses were like threads of gold, her blue eyes rivalled the colour of the sky on the balmiest summer day, and her smile was as radiant as the sunshine itself.

She was learned and clever, too, and her goodness of heart gained for her as great a renown as her peerless beauty. Despite all this, Princess Solima was not happy. Indeed, she was wretched to despondency, and her melancholy weighed heavily upon her father.

"What ails you, my precious daughter?" he asked her a hundred times, but she made no answer.

She just sat and silently moped. She did not waste away, which puzzled the physicians, but neither did she look healthy, which surprised her attendants, and she did not weep, which astonished herself. But she felt as if her heart had grown heavy, as if there was no use in anything.

The king squared his shoulders to show his determination and summoned his magicians and wizards and sorcerers and commanded them to perform their arts and solve the mystery of the illness of Princess Solima. A strange crew they were, ranged in a semi-circle before the king. There was the renowned astrologer from Egypt, a little man with a humpback. There was the mixer of mysterious potions from China, a long, lank yellow man, with tiny eyes. There too was the alchemist from Arabia, a scowling man with his face almost concealed by whiskers. There was a Greek and a Persian and a Phoenician, each with some special knowledge and fearfully anxious to display it. They all set to work.

One studied the stars, another concocted a sweet-smelling fluid, a third retired to the woods and thought deeply, a fourth made abstruse calculations with diagrams and figures, a fifth questioned the princess' handmaidens, and a sixth conceived the brilliant notion of talking with the princess herself. He was certainly an original wizard, and he learned more than all the others.

Then they met in consultation and talked foreign languages and pretended very seriously to understand one another. One said the stars were in opposition, another said he had gazed into a crystal and had seen a glow-worm chasing a hippopotamus which a third interpreted as meaning the princess would die if the glow-worm won the race.

"Rubbish!" exclaimed the magician who had spoken to the princess, "likewise stuff and nonsense and the equivalent thereof in the seventy unknown languages."

That was an impertinent comment on their divinations, and so they listened seriously.

"The princess," he said, "is just tired. That is a disease which will become popular and fashionable as the world grows older and more people amass riches. She is sick of being waited on hand and foot and bowed down to and all that sort of thing. She has never been allowed to romp as a child, to choose her own companions and the rest of it. Therefore, she is bored with all the etcetera's. The case is comprehensible and comprehensive: it needs the exercise of imagination stimulated by prescience, conscience, patience...."

The others yawned and began to collect dictionaries, and fearing that they might be tempted to fling them at him after they had found the meaning of his big words, he ceased.

"I agree," said the president of the assembly, the oldest wizard, "only I diagnose the disease in simpler form. The princess is in love."

That set them all jabbering together, and they finally agreed to report to the king that the time had arrived when the princess should marry, so that she should be able to go away to a new land, amid other people and different scenes.

The king agreed reluctantly, for he dearly loved his daughter and wished her to remain with him always if possible. Heralds and messengers were sent out far and wide, and very soon a procession of suitors for the princess' hand began to file past the lady. They were princes of all shapes and sizes, of all complexions and colours. Some were resplendent with jewels, while others were followed by retinues of slaves bearing gifts. A few entered the competition by proxy, that is, they sent somebody else to see the lady first and pronounce judgment upon her. These she dismissed summarily, declaring that they were disqualified by the rules of fair play.

When all the entrants had been inspected by the king, he said to his daughter, "Pick the one you love the best, Solima dear."

"None," she answered promptly.

"Dear, dear me, that is very awkward. We shall have to return the entrance fees, I mean the presents," he said.

That prospect did not seem to worry the princess in the least, nor did her father's appeal not to belittle him in the eyes of his fellow monarchs have the slightest effect on her.

"At least," he said, growing impatient, "tell me what you do want."

"I will marry any man," she replied, while he wondered gravely what else she could have said, "who is not such a fool as to think himself the only person in the world who is of consequence."

The king was not without wisdom, and he knew that this remark is foolish, or sensible, according to the mood in which it is said, and the thoughts behind it.

"You do not regard any one of the princes," the king said gently, "as worthy of..."

"Any woman," interrupted his daughter. "Listen, my father, you have tried to make me happy always and until recently you have succeeded. I wish to obey you in all things, even in the choice of a husband. Would you really have me marry any one of these fools? Don't be angry. Did anyone reveal a gleam of wisdom, or common-sense? Were they not all just ridiculous fops? Let me explain...

"There was Prince Hafiz who talked only of his wars, of the men and women and children that his soldiers had butchered. The soldiers fought and Prince Hafiz posed before me as a warrior and hero. I will not be queen in a land where people cannot live in peace.

"Then there was Prince Aziz who boasted that he spends all his life with his horses and dogs and falcons in the hunting field. He knows the needs of beasts, but not of men. I will not be the bride of a prince who allows his subjects to starve in wretchedness and poverty while he enjoys himself with the slaughter of wild beasts.

"Prince Guzman had nothing else to impart to me but his taste in jewels and dress. Prince Abdul knew exactly how many bottles of wine he drank daily, but he could not tell me how many schools there were in his city. Prince Hassan had not the slightest notion how the majority of his people lived, whether by trading, or thieving, or working, or begging."

King Zuliman listened intently. This was a singular speech for a princess, but reason told him this was profound wisdom.

"Oh, I am tired," burst out Princess Solima, in tears. "I have no desire for life if to be a ruler over men and women and children means that you must take no interest in their welfare. My father, listen. I will not be queen in a land where the king thinks the people live only to make him great. I shall be proud and happy to reign where the king understands that it is his duty to make his people happy and his country prosperous and peaceful."

The king left his daughter, and, deeply concerned, sought his wizards.

"My daughter has been born thousands of years before her time," he declared, petulantly. "The stars have played a trick on me, and have sent me my great-great-great-great ever so much great granddaughter out of her turn."

The magicians did not laugh at this. They thought it a wonderfully sage remark, and after much mysterious whispering among themselves and consultation of old books, and gazing into crystals, they informed the king that the stars foretold that Princess Solima would marry a poor man!

They flattered themselves on their cleverness in arriving at this conclusion, which they deduced from the princess' contempt for princes.

King Zuliman's patience was exhausted by this time. In a towering rage, he told his daughter what the wizards had said, and when she merely said, "How nice," he swore he would imprison her in his fortress in the sea.

His majesty meant it, too, and at once had the fortress, which stood on a tiny island miles from land, luxuriously furnished and fitted up for his daughter's reception. There she was conveyed secretly one night, but to her father's disgust she made no protest.

"I shall be free for a while," she said, "of all the absurd flummery of the palace."

II

The people were sad when the princess disappeared. She had been good and kind to them, had understood them, and they did not know whether she had died, or had deserted them without a word of farewell, though that was hardly possible. All that they knew was that the king suddenly became morose and sullen. Strangely enough, he began to take an interest in the poor. He asked them funny questions, for a king. How did they earn money? What was their occupation? Had they any pleasures? And what were their thoughts?

Young people laughed, but old men said the king intended to promote laws which would do good. Anyway, the king's interest did make his subjects happier, and the officers of state became very busy with projects and schemes for improving trade, providing work and for educating children.

"They do say," remarked one old woman, who kept an apple stall in the marketplace, "that a law will be passed that the sun should shine every day, and that it should never rain on the days of the market. Ah, that will be good," and she rubbed her hands at the prospect of not having to crouch under a leaky awning when the rain came pelting down, or over a tiny fire in a brass bowl in the winter, to thaw her frozen and numbed hands.

Even the labourers in the fields, who were mainly dull-witted people with no learning whatsoever, heard the news, and they actually pondered over it and wondered whether it meant that they would never more be hungry and wretchedly clad.

One who thought deeply was a shepherd lad. He loved to bask lazily in the sun, to listen to the birds chirruping, and to all the sounds of the air and the fields and the forests. He seemed to understand that the murmuring of the brooks on a warm day was like a gentle cradle song lulling him to sleep. On a day when the wind howled, its sulky growl as it dashed over the stones warned him that floods might come, and that he must move his flocks to safer ground.

"I wonder," he mused, "if I shall learn to read the written word and even to pen it myself. I could then write the song of the brook and the birds, so that others should know it."

And musing thus, he fell asleep. He slept longer than usual, and when he awoke, he was alarmed to see that the sun had set. Darkness was falling fast, and he had his flock to see safely home. The cows and sheep had begun to collect themselves as a matter of habit, and it was their noise that woke him. They were already trudging the well-known route, and all he had to do in following was to see that none strayed, or tumbled into the brook.

All went well until he came in sight of home. Then a huge bird, a ziz, bigger than several houses, appeared in the sky and swooped down on the cows and sheep.

The shepherd beat the monster off as long as he could with a big stick, while the frightened animals scampered hastily homeward. The ziz however, was evidently determined not to be balked of its prey. It dug its talons deep into the flanks of an ox that had stampeded in the wrong direction and was lagging behind the others.

The poor animal bellowed in pain, and the shepherd, rushing to the rescue, seized it by the forelegs as it was being raised from the ground. Curling his leg round the slender trunk of a tree, the young man began a struggle with the ziz. The mighty bird, its eyes glowing like two signal lamps, tried to strike at him with his tremendous beak, one stroke of which would have been fatal.

In the fast gathering darkness it missed, fortunately for the shepherd, but the thrust of the beak caught the upper part of the tree trunk. It snapped under the blow, and the shepherd was compelled to release his hold. He still gripped the forelegs of the ox tightly, but with nothing now to hold it back, the great bird had no difficulty in rising into the air. Before he fully grasped what had happened, the shepherd found himself high above the trees.

To release his hold would have meant destruction. He held on grimly, clutching the legs of the ox with all his might, and even swinging up his feet to grip the hind-legs of the animal.

Higher and higher the ziz rose into the air, spreading its vast wings majestically, and flying silently and swiftly over the land. It made the shepherd giddy to glance down at the ground scurrying rapidly past far below him. So he closed his eyes, but opening them again for a moment, he was horrified to notice that the bird was now flying over the sea on which the moon was shining with silvery radiance. With a heavy sigh he gave himself up for lost, and began to consider whether it would be better to release his hold and fall down and be drowned, rather than be devoured by the gigantic bird.

Before he could make up his mind, the bird stopped, and the shepherd was bumped down on something with such violence that for a moment he was stunned. Looking around, when he regained his senses, he saw that he was on the top of a tower in the sea. Beside him was the carcass of the ox. Above them stood the ziz, its eyes glowing like twin fires, its beak thrust down to strike.

With a quick movement, the shepherd drew a knife which he carried in his girdle, and struck at the opening of the descending beak. The bird uttered a shrill cry of pain as the knife pierced its tongue, and in a few moments it had disappeared in the air. So swift was its flight that almost instantly it was a mere speck in the moonlit sky.

Thoroughly exhausted, the shepherd slept until awakened by the sound of a voice. Opening his eyes, he saw that the sun had risen. Above him stood a woman of ravishing beauty. He sprang to his feet and bowed low.

"Who are you?" asked Princess Solima, for she it was. "And tell me how you came here with this carcass of an ox, so distant from the land, so high up as this tower in the sea?"

"Of a truth I scarcely know," answered the shepherd. "It may be that I am bewitched, or dreaming, for my adventure passes all belief," and he related it.

The princess made no comment, but motioned to him that he should follow her. He did so and she placed food before him. He was ravenously hungry and did full justice to the meal. Then she led him to the bath chamber.

"Wash and robe yourself," she said, giving him some clothes, "and then I have much to inquire of you."

The shepherd felt ever so much better when he had bathed, and then attired in the strange garments she had given him, he appeared before the princess.

She gazed at him so long and searchingly that he blushed in confusion.

"You are fair to look upon and of manly stature," said the princess.

The shepherd could only stammer a reply, but after a while he said, "Fair lady, who and what you are I know not. Such beauty as yours is the right of princesses only. I am but a poor shepherd."

"And may not a shepherd be handsome?" she asked. "Tell me, who has laid down a law that only royal personages may be fair to behold? I have seen princes of vile countenance."

She stopped suddenly, for she did not wish to betray her secret. They sat in a little room in the tower, unknown to the many guards down below, and, although the shepherd protested, the princess waited on him herself, bringing him food, and cushions on which he could rest that night.

Next morning they ascended the tower together.

"I come here every morning," said the princess.

"Why?" the shepherd asked.

"To see if my husband has come," was the answer.

"Who is he?" asked the shepherd.

The princess laughed.

"I don't know," she said. "Some mornings when I have stood here and grieved at my loneliness, I have felt inclined to make a vow that I would marry the first man who came here."

The shepherd was silent. Then he looked boldly into the princess' eyes and said, "You have told me I am the first man who has come to you. I am emboldened to declare my love for you, a feeling that swept over me the moment my eyes beheld you. Who you are, what you are, I don't know, nor do I care. Shall we be husband and wife?"

The princess gave him her hand. "It is ordained," she said, and thus their troth was plighted.

"We cannot remain here forever," said the princess, presently. "Can you, husband of my heart's choice, devise some means of escape?"

He looked down at the carcass of the ox thoughtfully for a few moments. "I have it," he exclaimed, excitedly. "It is a safe assumption that the monster bird that brought me will return for his meal. He can then carry us away. If the heavens approve," he said, fervently, "thus it shall be."

That very night the ziz returned and feasted on the ox, and while it was fully occupied appeasing its hunger, the shepherd managed to attach strong ropes to its legs. To this he attached a large basket in which he and his bride made themselves comfortable with cushions. Nor did they forget to take a store of food.

Toward morning the ziz rose slowly into the air, and the lovers clutched each other tightly as the basket spun round and round. The giant bird did not seem to notice its burden at all, and after a moment it began a swift flight over the sea. After many hours a city became visible, and as it was approached the shepherd could note the excitement caused by the appearance of the ziz. The bird was getting tired, and having at last noticed the weight tied to its feet was evidently seeking to get rid of it.

Flying low it dashed the basket against a tower. The occupants feared they might be killed, but suddenly the cords snapped, the basket came to rest, and the bird flew swiftly away.

No sooner had the shepherd extricated himself and his bride from the basket, than armed guards appeared. At sight of the princess they lowered their weapons and fell upon their faces.

"Inform my father I have returned," she said, and they immediately rose to do her bidding.

"Do you know where you are?" asked the shepherd.

"Yes, this is the king's palace," was the reply.

Soon the king appeared, and with almost hysterical joy he embraced his daughter. "I am happy to see you again," he cried. "I crave your pardon for locking you away in the sea fortress. You shall tell me all your adventures." Then he caught sight of the shepherd. "Who is this?" he demanded.

"Your son-in-law, my husband," said the princess, her joy showing in her bright eyes.

"What prince are you?" asked the king.

"A prince among men," answered the princess quickly. "A man without riches, who comes from the people and will teach us their needs and how to rule them."

The king bowed to the inevitable. He blessed his son-in-law and daughter, appointed them to rule over a province, and they settled down to make everybody thoroughly happy, contented and prosperous.

The Legend Of Ara And Semiramis

This story has been adapted from Louis A. Boettiger's version of the same tale that originally appeared in Armenian Legends and Festivals, published in 1920 by University of Minnesota, Minneapolis.

Ara was incredibly beautiful, and Semiramis, having heard about his beauty for many years, desired to possess him. However, she refrained from taking any action due to her fear of Ninus, the protector of Armenia. After Ninus's death, the queen sent messengers to Ara, offering gifts, making promises of wealth, and urging him to come to Nineveh. She proposed that he either marry her and rule over all that Ninus had possessed or fulfil her desire and return peacefully to Armenia with numerous gifts.

After repeated rejections of her messengers, Semiramis grew angry. Gathering her army, she swiftly marched to Armenia. The battle took place on the plain of Ara, later named Ararat after him. Despite the queen's explicit orders to her generals to find a way to spare Ara's life, the Armenian king was killed. Among the fallen bodies, Semiramis discovered Ara's corpse and commanded her servants to place it in an upper chamber of her castle.

When the Armenian army rose again to drive away the enemy and avenge Ara's death, the queen proclaimed, "I have commanded the gods to lick his wounds, and he shall live again." Despite her attempts at witchcraft and charms to revive Ara, the body started to decay. Semiramis ordered her servants to cast the corpse into a deep pit and cover it.

In secret, she dressed up one of her men and spread a proclamation among the people, "The gods have licked Ara and have brought him back to life again, fulfilling our prayers and desires. Henceforth, they shall be glorified and worshipped by us, as givers of joy and fulfillers of desires."

She erected a statue to the gods, creating an illusion that they had resurrected Ara. This news spread throughout the entire country of Armenia, satisfying the people and putting an end to the fighting.

The Assyrian queen took the twelve-year-old son of the king and appointed him ruler over Armenia. She named him Ara, in memory of her love for Ara the Beautiful.

The One Good Giant: St. Christopher

This story has been adapted from Henry Wysham Lanier's version of the same tale that originally appeared in A Book of Giants, published in 1922 by E. P. Dutton and Company, New York. This is traditionally thought of as a tale originating in what is now Syria.

Listen to the tale in the "Golden Legend" of the giant Syrian, fair of face and spirit, who converted countless thousands of unbelievers to the faith before becoming a martyr during the persecution by the Byzantine emperor in the third century after Christ's birth. Never before or since has a patron saint of ferrymen sprung forth like this from "the seed of the giant" that produced Og, King of Bashan, and Goliath of Gath.

Christopher, before his baptism, was named Reprobus, but later he was called Christopher, meaning "bearing Christ," due to the four ways he carried Christ. He bore Him on his shoulders by conveying and leading, in his body by making it lean, in his mind by devotion, and in his mouth by confession and prediction.

Christopher belonged to the Canaanite lineage, and he was of great stature, with a terrifying appearance. He stood twelve cubits tall, and according to some histories, when he served and lived with the king of Canaan, he decided to seek the greatest prince in the world, whom he would serve and obey. He journeyed until he reached a mighty king, widely renowned as the greatest in the world. When the king saw him, he welcomed him into his service and had him dwell in his court. Once, a minstrel sang a song in which the devil was mentioned frequently. The king, a Christian man, made the sign of the cross on his face upon hearing the devil's name.

Observing this, Christopher wondered about the significance of the sign and why the king made it. When he inquired, and the king hesitated to explain, Christopher said, "If you do not tell me, I will no longer stay with you."

The king then revealed, "Whenever I hear the devil named, I fear that he may have power over me. I make this sign to protect myself from harm."

Christopher responded, "Do you believe the devil has power to harm you? Then the devil is mightier and greater than you. I am deceived in my hope and purpose, for I had thought I had found the mightiest and greatest Lord of the world. I commend you to God, for I will seek Him to be my Lord, and I will be His servant." Christopher departed from the king and hurried to seek the devil.

While passing through a vast desert, he encountered a group of knights, and a cruel and horrible devil-knight approached him, asking where he was going. Christopher identified himself, and the knight was pleased. Christopher willingly bound himself to be the knight's perpetual servant, taking him as his master and Lord.

As they walked together along a common path, they came across an upright cross. The moment the devil saw the cross, he became frightened and fled, abandoning the right path. Instead, he led Christopher through a harsh desert. Christopher, puzzled, asked why the devil had hesitated, left the high and clear path, and taken such a roundabout route through the desert. The devil refused to explain.

Christopher then told him, "If you won't tell me, I'll leave you immediately and serve you no more."

Reluctantly, the devil revealed, "There was a man called Christ who was crucified, and when I see His sign, I am terrified and flee from it wherever I encounter it."

Christopher responded, "Then He is greater and mightier than you if you fear His sign. I realize I have laboured in vain, not finding the greatest Lord of the world. I will no longer serve you. Go your way, for I will seek Christ."

After a long search for Christ, Christopher finally arrived in a vast desert, where a hermit resided. The hermit preached about Jesus Christ, diligently instructing Christopher in the faith. He told him, "The king you desire to serve requires a service that involves frequent fasting."

Christopher replied, "Ask of me something else, for I cannot do what you ask."

The hermit said, "Then you must keep vigil and offer many prayers."

Christopher replied, "I don't know what that is. I cannot do such a thing."

The hermit then said, "Do you know of a river where many have perished?"

Christopher affirmed, "I know it well."

The hermit continued, "Because you are noble, tall, and strong, you shall stay by that river. You will carry everyone who needs to pass, a service that will be fitting for our Lord Jesus Christ, whom you desire to serve. I hope He will reveal Himself to you."

Christopher said, "Certainly, I can perform this service, and I promise to do it for Him."

Christopher went to the river, made it his dwelling, and used a large pole instead of a staff to support himself in the water. He tirelessly carried people across the river. He continued this service for many days.

One time, as he slept in his dwelling, he heard a child's voice calling him, saying, "Christopher, come out and carry me across." He woke up, went out, but found no one. Upon returning to his house, he heard the same voice again and ran out, finding nobody.

The third time he was called, he went there and found a child by the riverbank, politely asking him to carry him across. Christopher lifted the child onto his shoulders, took his pole, and entered the river to cross. The water swelled and rose as he went deeper, and the child became as heavy as lead. The farther he went, the more the water increased, and the child became heavier. Christopher, fearing drowning, struggled but eventually made it across. Setting the child on the ground, he said, "Child, you have put me in great peril. You weighed almost as much as if I had the entire world on my shoulders. I couldn't bear a greater burden."

And the child answered, "Christopher, don't be surprised, for you have not only borne the weight of the entire world but also carried Him who created and made the entire world upon your shoulders. I am Jesus Christ, the king, whom you serve in this work. And because you know that what I say is true, plant your staff in the ground near your house, and by morning, you shall see it bearing flowers and fruit." And immediately, he vanished from Christopher's sight.

Christopher placed his staff in the earth, and when he woke up the next morning, he found his staff resembling a palm tree, adorned with flowers, leaves, and dates.

Christopher entered the city of Lysia but couldn't understand their language. He prayed to the Lord to grant him understanding, and his prayer was answered. While he was in prayer, the judges assumed he was a fool and left him there. When Christopher understood the language, he covered his face and went to the place where Christians were being martyred. He comforted them in the Lord, and the judges struck him in the face. Christopher responded, "If I were not a Christian, I would avenge my injury."

Christopher planted his rod in the earth, praying for it to bear flowers and fruit to convert the people. And indeed, it happened. He converted eight thousand men.

The king sent two knights to bring him, but finding him praying, they dared not interrupt him. Later, the king sent two more knights, who joined Christopher in prayer. When Christopher asked them what they sought, they said, "The king has sent us to bind you and to lead you to him." Christopher replied, "Whether bound or unbound, if I wanted to go with you, you could not lead me. But I will go with you."

He converted the knights to the faith, and they led him bound to the king. Seeing Christopher, the king was frightened, fell off his seat, and was raised again by his servants. The king inquired about Christopher's name and country.

Christopher replied, "Before I was baptized, I was named Reprobus, and after baptism, I am Christopher. Once I was a Canaanite, but now I am a Christian man."

The king mocked his name, calling it foolish.

Christopher retorted, "You are rightly called Dagnus, a follower of the devil and fellow of the devil. Your gods are made by human hands."

The king threatened Christopher with great pains and torments if he did not sacrifice to the gods. Christopher refused, was sent to prison, and the king beheaded the knights who had converted because of him.

The king then sent two women to tempt Christopher with sin. Christopher prayed, and when forced by them, he stood up and asked, "Why are you here?"

Afraid of his demeanour, they said, "Holy saint of God, have pity on us, so we may believe in the God you preach."

The king allowed them to speak with Christopher. They told him the king's threat, but Christopher assured them, "You will perish unless you sacrifice to the gods." To prove his point, they destroyed the idols in the temple. The king executed the women, but Christopher remained unharmed.

Despite the king's various attempts, including burning, melting iron, and shooting arrows, Christopher remained unharmed. Finally, he was beheaded. The king, blinded by an arrow, sought a cure from Christopher's blood, and upon applying it, he was healed. The king then converted to God, ordering death for anyone who spoke against God or St. Christopher.

The Higgledy-Piggledy Palace

This story has been adapted from Gertrude Landa's version of the same tale that originally appeared in Jewish Fairy Tales and Legends, published in 1943 by Bloch Publishing Co. Inc., New York.

Sarah was the wife of the patriarch Abraham, and the great mother of the Jewish people. She was the most beautiful woman who ever lived. Everybody who saw her marvelled at the dazzling radiance of her countenance. They stood spellbound before the glorious light that shone in her eyes and the wondrous clearness of her complexion. This greatly troubled Abraham when he fled from Canaan to Egypt. It was disconcerting to have crowds of travellers gazing at his wife as if she were something more than human. Besides, he feared that the Egyptians would seize Sarah for the king's harem.

So, after much meditation, he concealed his wife in a big box. When he arrived at the Egyptian frontier, the customs officials asked him what it contained.

"Barley," he replied.

"You say that because the duty on barley is the lowest," they said. "The box must surely be packed with wheat."

"I will pay the duty on wheat," said Abraham, who was most anxious they should not open the box.

The officials were surprised, for, as a rule, people endeavoured to avoid paying the duties. "If you are so ready to pay the higher tax," they said, "the box must contain something of greater value. Perhaps it contains spices."

Abraham intimated his readiness to pay the duty on spices.

"Oh, Oh!" laughed the officers. "Here is a strange person ready to pay heavy dues. He must be anxious to conceal something, gold, perchance."

"I will pay the duty on gold," said Abraham, quietly.

The officers were now completely bewildered. "Our highest duty," said their chief, "is on precious stones, and since you decline to open the box, we must demand the tax on the costliest gems."

"I will pay it," said Abraham, simply.

The officers could not understand this at all, and after consulting among themselves, they decided that the box must be opened. "It may contain something highly dangerous," they argued.

Abraham protested, but he was arrested by the guards and the box forced open. When Sarah was revealed, the officials stepped back in amazement and admiration.

"Indeed, a rare jewel," said the chief.

It was immediately decided to send Sarah to the king. When Pharaoh beheld her, he was enraptured. She was simply dressed in the garments of a peasant woman, with no adornment and no jewels, and yet the king thought he had never seen a woman so entrancingly beautiful. When he saw Abraham, however, his brow clouded.

"Who is this man?" he demanded of Sarah.

Fearing that he might be imprisoned, or even put to death if she acknowledged him as her husband, Sarah replied that he was her brother.

Pharaoh felt relieved. He smiled on Abraham and greeted him pleasantly. "Your sister is exceedingly fair to gaze upon," he said, "and beautiful. She has bewitched me by her matchless charm. She shall become the favourite of my harem. I will recompense you well for your loss of her. You shall be loaded with gifts."

Abraham was too wise to betray the anger that surged in his heart. "Courage, my beloved," he whispered to Sarah. "The good God will not forsake us."

He made pretence of agreeing to Pharaoh's suggestion, and the chief steward of the king gave him an abundant store of gold and silver and jewels, also sheep and oxen and camels. Abraham was conducted to a beautiful palace, where many slaves attended him and bowed before him, for one on whom the monarch had showered favours was a great man in the land of Pharaoh. Left alone, Abraham began to pray most devoutly.

Meanwhile, Sarah was led into a gorgeous apartment where the queen's own attendants were ordered to array her in the richest of the royal garments. Then she was brought before Pharaoh who dismissed all the attendants.

"I desire to be alone with you," said the king to Sarah. "I have much to say to you, and I long to feast my eyes on those features of rare beauty."

But Sarah shrank from him. To her, he appeared ugly and loathsome. His smile was a vicious leer, and his voice sounded like a harsh croak.

"Fear not," he said, trying to speak tenderly and kindly. "I will do you no harm. No, I will load you with honours. I will grant any request that you make."

"Then let me go," said Sarah, quickly. "I desire nothing other than that you should permit me to depart with my brother."

"You jest," said Pharaoh. "That cannot be. I will make you queen," he cried, passionately and he made a move toward her.

"Stop!" cried Sarah. "If you approach one step nearer...."

Pharaoh interrupted her with a laugh. To threaten a king was so funny that he could not refrain from a hoarse cackle. But Sarah had become suddenly silent. She was looking not at him, but behind him. Pharaoh turned, but observed nothing. He could not see what Sarah saw, for she saw a figure, a spirit, clutching a big stick.

"Come," said the king, "don't be foolish. I cannot be angry with a creature so fair as you are. But it is not wise to utter threats to one who wears a crown."

Sarah made no reply. She was no longer afraid. She knew that her prayers, and those of Abraham, had been answered, and that no harm would befall her. Pharaoh mistook her silence and advanced toward her. As he did so, however, he felt a tremendous blow on the head. He was stunned for a moment. On recovering himself he looked around the room, but could see nothing. Sarah continued to stand motionless.

"Strange," muttered Pharaoh. "I... I thought someone had entered the room."

Again he moved toward Sarah, and once more he received a staggering blow, this time on the shoulder. It was only by a great effort of will that he did not cry out in pain. He concluded he must have been seized by some sudden illness, but after a moment he felt better and bravely tried to smile at Sarah.

"I… I just thought of something most important," said he, attempting to offer some explanation for nearly toppling over in an undignified manner. He stood nearer to Sarah and began to raise his hand to touch her.

"If you lay a finger on me, it will be at your peril," exclaimed Sarah, her eyes flashing angrily.

"Pshaw!" he cried, losing patience, and he raised his hand. This time the cudgel of the spirit invisible to Pharaoh did not strike him: it came down gently and rested lightly on the king's out-stretched arm. And Pharaoh could not move it. He grew pale and trembled.

"Are you a witch?" he gasped at last.

Sarah was so angry when she heard this insult that she flashed a signal with her eyes to the spirit, and the latter plied his cudgel lustily about the king's head and shoulders, making the monarch break out in most unkingly howls of pain.

"Your pardon, your pardon, I crave," he managed to scream. "I mean not what I said. I am ill, very ill. My body aches. My arm is paralyzed."

The cudgelling ceased and Pharaoh was able to move his arm. He writhed in agony, for he was bruised all over. He rushed hastily away, saying he would return on the morrow. Sarah found herself locked in, but she was not disturbed again.

Pharaoh, however, had further adventures. The spirit was in merry mood and had a night's entertainment at the king's expense. No sooner did the king lie down upon his bed than the spirit tilted it and sent him sprawling on the floor. Whenever Pharaoh tried to lie down the same thing happened. He went from one room to another, but all efforts at rest were unavailing. Every bed rejected him and every chair and couch did the same, although when he commanded others to lie down they did so quite comfortably. He tried lying down with one of his attendants, but while the latter was able to remain undisturbed, Pharaoh found himself bodily lifted, stood upon his head, spun around and then rolled over on the ground.

His physicians could provide no remedy, his magicians, hastily summoned from their own slumbers, could afford no explanation, and Pharaoh spent a terrible night wandering from room to room and up and down the corridors, where the corners seemed to go out of their way to bump against him and the stairs seemed to go down when he wanted to walk up, and vice-versa. Such a higgledy-piggledy palace was never seen. Worse still, with the first streak of dawn he noticed that he was smitten with leprosy.

Hastily he sent for Abraham and said, "Who and what you are I do not know. You and your sister have brought a plague. I desired to make her my queen, but now I say to you this: Rid me of this leprosy and go away with your sister. I will bestow riches on you, but get gone, and speedily."

With a magic jewel which he wore on his breast, Abraham restored Pharaoh to health, and then departed with Sarah. These final words he said to Pharaoh, "Sarah is not my sister, but my wife. I give you this warning. Should your descendants at any time seek to persecute our descendants, then our God, the One God of the universe, will surely punish the king with plague again."

And, many years afterward, as you read in the Bible, the prediction came true.

The Legend Of Vahakn

This story has been adapted from Louis A. Boettiger's version of the same tale that originally appeared in Armenian Legends and Festivals, published in 1920 by University of Minnesota, Minneapolis.

The legend of Vahakn, king and god of Armenians, is very clearly attributable to the Greek period, which followed the Persian conquest under Xerxes. Vahakn was deified because of his great valour and made the fire-god of the Armenian people. He was called "Vishapakagh," uprooter of dragons since he cleared Armenia of monsters and saved it from evil influences. His exploits were known in the abode of the gods as well as in Armenia. The most famous of them was the theft of corn from the barns of King Barsham of Assyria, from whom he ran away and tried to hide in heaven. Because of the ears he dropped in his rapid flight, there arose the Milky Way which is called in Armenian the "track of the corn stealer."

Concerning the birth of the king, the legends tell this story…

Heaven and earth were in turmoil, and the red waters were agitated. Within the water, a red reed was also in turmoil. Smoke and flames emanated from the reed, and from the flames emerged a child with fiery hair, a beard of flames, and sun-like eyes.

The legend goes on to tell of the child's battle with dragons, likening his heroic deeds to those of Hercules. Some claim he was a god, and a grand statue of him stood in Georgia, worshipped with sacrifices.

Vahakn's spouse was Astghik, the goddess of beauty and a moon personification.

The narrative contains a touch of humour, akin to the Greeks' ability to mock their gods. The image of a bearded god, a dragon slayer with flaming hair and sun-like eyes, stealing corn from the Assyrian king and dropping ears from his shoulders in a hurried escape across the heavens is delightfully humorous. The legend's rich imaginative quality, especially in the birth song, the open anthropomorphism, and the parallels between the Greek fire-god Vulcan and the Armenian fire-god Vahakn, both married to goddesses of beauty, unmistakably reveal its origin in Greek mythology.

Dragon-Child And Sun-Child

This story has been adapted from Abraham G. Seklemian's version of the same tale that originally appeared in The Golden Maiden and Other Folk Tales and Fairy Stories Told in Armenia, published in 1898 by The Helman-Taylor Company, New York. This tale is based on earlier work undertaken by Ohannes Chatschumian, who, before his death, had begun a compilation of 'Armenian' folklore for Miss Alice Fletcher. These 'Armenian' tales themselves originated in the Byzantine peasant tradition that developed over the preceding fifteen hundred years.

There was once a King who had no children, and whose life was very desolate. He asked the advice of all the doctors and learned men of his realm to relieve him of his trouble, but it was of no avail. In order to forget his dejected condition, he gave his time to hunting. One day, as he was walking in the forest he saw a snake coiled in the sun, surrounded by its little ones. For a long time he gazed wistfully at this family circle, and recognizing that his condition was inferior to that of the reptile parent, he sighed deeply and complained against Heaven, saying, "Oh Heaven! Have I not so much value before you as this reptile, that you torment me by denying to me offspring and happiness?"

He never forgot the sight of this snake-family.

One day, when the grief of the King was heavier than ever before, a child came to the palace, but it was a monster, half man and half dragon. They could not kill the monster because it was of royal birth, so they cast the Dragon-child into a dry well, where they fed him by giving him a skinful of goat's milk every day. Soon the Dragon-child grew and required meat for his diet. Then they threw him, every week, a tender girl, and when he grew older, they gave him a maiden to devour. Every house of the land furnished a maiden for the Dragon-child.

It became the turn of a poor man who, being a widower, had a daughter from his former wife, and had married a widow who had a daughter of her own. The husband said that they must cast the wife's daughter to the Dragon-child, but his wife insisted that they must cast the husband's daughter. The woman's will was followed and so the stepmother prepared her stepdaughter to be cast to the Dragon-child on the following day. The maiden was very beautiful and graceful. She wept all night and prayed God to pity her.

At midnight she heard someone speak to her in her dreams, saying, "Maiden, do not be afraid of being thrown down to the Dragon-child. Tell your father to send with you three skinfuls of the milk of a black goat, and take a knife for yourself. Let your father wrap you in a bull's skin and lower you and the milk by a rope into the well. When the Dragon-child bids you come out from the bull's skin in order that he may devour you, tell him to come out from the dragon's skin, that you may bathe him with milk. When he comes out, cut the bull's skin with your knife and come out of the skin and bathe him."

On the following morning the maiden told her dream to her father, who got the required things ready, at the same time praying to Heaven that what the maiden had dreamed might come true. The maiden being lowered into the well, the Dragon-child told her to come out of the bull's skin, to which the maiden answered as she was advised. Thereupon in its fury, the dragon's skin burst, and there issued from it a handsome lad. The maiden cut the bull's skin with her knife in a hurry, but in her haste she fell down, and one of her front teeth was broken. She bathed the lad with goat's milk and he became a sound, gallant youth, who at once expressed his gratitude to her for releasing him from his horrible bondage.

Just then the maiden's father came to the mouth of the well, to see whether her dream was true or false, and perceiving them, ran to inform the King, who hastened to the spot accompanied by the Queen and his peers. They drew the Dragon-child and his deliverer from the well with great joy and ceremony. They celebrated a wedding festival for forty days and nights, and the youth and the maiden loved one another and were married.

It came to pass, after a time, that on account of a war the Dragon-child had to go away from home. When he was about to depart he asked his mother not to send his bride away, not even to her father's, in case some misfortune should befall her. The Queen promised. But a thousand devils had entered the heart of the bride's stepmother, who was jealous of her good luck. She came and invited the bride to their house, saying that both she and her husband were longing to see her. When this was refused she sent her husband, who urgently entreated the Queen to send his daughter to his house at least for one day. The Queen thought there could be no harm in this, and so she let the bride go.

The stepmother took her daughter and the bride for a walk on the seashore. When they came there she said to them, "Daughters, let us bathe."

They entered the sea to bathe. The wicked woman, pretending to help the bride, took her toward the deep sea, where she gave her a violent push and she was caught by the waves and was drawn by the current out to the open sea. When she was sure that the bride had been drowned, she hastened to the shore with her own daughter, and putting the bride's dress on the latter, sent her to the King's palace as the true bride.

For a long time the true bride struggled against the violent waves, and was saved from being drowned by catching hold of an empty cask which happened to float near her. The wind blew from the shore, and the current carried the cask and the maiden away to the open sea. For three days and nights she floated with the cask, and then she was cast upon an uninhabited shore. She walked for a time on the coast, but saw no sign of a human being. She was hungry, naked and very tired.

The first thing she did was to gather rushes and moss and weave for herself something like an apron to hide her nakedness. She then gathered wild berries and ate, and quenched her thirst from a brook nearby. While she was lingering on the banks of the brook she noticed a small hut hidden among the bullrushes and weeds. Proceeding there, she looked in, and a lad was sleeping in the hut. She sat down near the door of the hut. Soon after sunset the lad awoke, and as he was coming out of the hut, he noticed the maiden.

Thinking that she was a fairy or a demon, he made upon his face the sign of the cross, at the same time stepping backward. But to his surprise, seeing that she did not vanish, he said to her, "Are you a fairy, a demon or a human being? Disclose yourself."

The maiden told him her story.

"My own story is as strange as yours," said the lad. "I was the only son of a rich man and had plenty to spend and enjoy. I led a dissipated life and went hunting every day. Once it happened that I did not shoot any game for three days in succession. I was enraged to the verge of madness, and wandered all the night. At daybreak my madness reached its climax, and I resolved to shoot the sun and drop him dead from his orbit so that darkness might cover the world, since I could take no game and have no pleasure. At once I grasped my bow and arrow, took aim at the sun, who had just lifted his shining face from behind the hills, and had hardly loosed the bowstring when I felt a blazing palm slap me in the face. A hand of fire took hold of my hair and cast me into this wilderness, and I heard an angry voice thundering at me from the overhanging clouds, declaring that I was cursed and should never see the light of the sun anymore. I thus remain abandoned here, and sleep in the hut all day while the sun shines, and go out only at night to procure food. If I go out of this hut after daybreak I am doomed to die a horrible death."

As fate had so strangely cast these two youthful beings into the same lonely place, they decided to live together, accepting one another as husband and wife. Thus she who had been the consort of the Dragon-child was now the companion of the Sun-child. The woman worked in the daytime, and the man at night, and so they earned their living. But soon married life brought a change upon the woman, who needed the help of others, and they decided that she must go to the parents of the Sun-child. The lad wrote the following letter to his parents:

'I herewith send you your daughter-in-law. Keep her and take care of her as my wife. But do not seek me, for I cannot see the sun, I

cannot come home, neither can I enter the city. If I do come I shall surely die, for I am cursed.'

Walking during the nights, and hiding himself in caves in daytime, the lad brought his wife to the vicinity of his parents' house, and himself went back to his lonely hut. The woman gave the letter to her father-in-law, and was accepted. The lad's father and mother hearing that their son was alive, said they would go and bring him, but the bride dissuaded them, saying that they would be the means of his death.

In the fullness of time the family was cheered by the birth of a son, which the young mother put in a cradle and rocked, singing to it melodious lullabies from the incidents of her own life. One night as the young mother was putting her baby to sleep, another voice was heard out in the darkness singing a melodious lullaby. The bride recognized the voice to be that of the Sun-child, who had come from such a great distance, being drawn by the love of the baby, but he could not enter. This was repeated several times until the bride's father and mother-in-law heard that somebody was in the habit of coming at night, and singing lullabies by turns with their daughter-in-law. Suspicion entered into their minds that the bride might have a lover who was making nightly calls on her.

The young woman, seeing that they were watching her with mistrust, said, "It is your son who comes and sings lullabies. The love which he bears for the baby draws him, but he cannot enter, for the moment you compel him to come in he dies."

"No, you are lying!" exclaimed her father and mother-in-law with rage. "There must be some foul play here. We will keep watch and catch the nightly visitor. If he proves to be our son, well and good. If not, woe to you."

That night they kept watch, and when the voice from outside was heard they ran and took hold of the man, and it was their son, who begged them, saying, "For Heaven's sake, let me go! If by the time the sun rises I am not hidden in my hut, I die. Spare my life; I am cursed!"

This sounded to his father and mother like deceit, and they kept him at home until daybreak. As soon as the first rays of the sun beamed from the East, the lad sank in the arms of his father and mother, and died. He died, but strange to say, his spirit did not depart from him entirely. They said he would revive at sunset, but it was not so. At night he remained in the same numbed state. The house was changed into a house of sorrow; but worse than that happened. He was not dead so that they could bury him and he was not alive so that they might talk with him or administer a remedy. The parents took stones and beat their own heads, they pulled their hair, and sat in ashes and sackcloth. They lamented and wailed, but it was all of no avail. One night the afflicted mother dreamed a dream in which this revelation was made to her:

'Get up, put on iron sandals, take in your hand an iron rod and travel toward the West, until your sandals are worn and your rod is broken. Wherever holes are opened in your sandals and your rod is broken, there you will find a remedy for your son.'

There is no limit to a mother's love and pity. As soon as she awoke in the morning she ordered the blacksmith to make her a pair of iron sandals and an iron rod, and she set out toward the West, walking day and night. She travelled through the countries of white men, red men, and black men. She passed through the lands of fairies, giants and genii. She went farther than beasts and birds would dare to go, for she had gone to the very limits of the earth. There she saw at a distance a palace built of blue marble, where she proceeded. Before the palace door the iron rod fell from her hand and was broken. She got out her sandals to shake off the dust, and they were worn and there was a hole in each. She said to herself, "It is here that I shall find a remedy for my son!"

She entered and passed through twelve courtyards in succession. Each courtyard was surrounded by four arches, where thousands of myriads of stars were sleeping. At the centre of each courtyard there was a marble pond with a stream of crystal water gushing from an orifice. There were no trees, no grass, no birds, no beasts, and no other creature. A deep silence was reigning everywhere. Upon the pond in the middle courtyard there were four golden arches, upon which there was a golden room of great splendour with a pearl bed in the centre. Near the window there was, sitting upon a golden throne, a Queen so fair and beautiful, that no human being can describe her loveliness. From head to foot she was covered with diamonds and her face beamed with rays of light. At sight of this grandeur the poor woman was greatly amazed. She turned pale and began to shiver like an autumn leaf before a cold blast from the North.

She fell upon her knees, and lifting her hands, was about to speak, when suddenly the Queen interrupted her, saying, "Human being, Heaven has never permitted a member of the human race to enter this palace before. As you are the first mortal who has been allowed to come so far, you must have some valid reason. From your appearance I judge that you are a mother and have some maternal grief. Tell it to me. Don't be afraid."

These words of the Queen encouraged the woman, who said, "Long live the Queen! Yes, I am a mother, and have travelled so far to ask the life of my only son."

And she told her story, to which the Queen made answer, "Your son was an evil boy. I am a mother myself. The Sun is my son, by whose living rays heaven and earth are illumined. Your son was so wicked that he wanted to shoot my son, the giver of life to the universe. All kinds of sins may be pardonable to a man, but a sin against the sole source of life is not pardonable. Your son was therefore doomed to be deprived of life. He is cursed. He will live, but not live. He will die, but not die."

"I am a mother," repeated the woman, "come to beg the life of my son. I have come so far that my iron sandals are worn out, and my iron rod is broken. I would willingly go still further if it were necessary. For the love you bear your son, O Queen of this luminous orb, devise a remedy for my grief!"

These words served to arouse the compassion of the Queen, who replied, "There are very many unworthy children who enjoy life simply because of their virtuous mothers. Let it be so with your son, O virtuous woman, who bear such great maternal love in your heart! Now, go hide yourself behind yonder stars. The day is growing towards evening and my son will soon be here. If you do not hide yourself you will be burned. The first thing he does after reaching this place is to dive in this pond. Then he comes to be nursed from my breast. Just then take a bottle full of the water of the pond where he has been washing, and carry it home. As soon as you sprinkle that water upon your son he will be healed."

Soon the Sun came embodied in flames. The Stars woke up and stood on their feet for a time to salute their mighty King. Then they scattered over the surface of the blue dome to twinkle in their respective orbits, because it was night. The Sun dove into the pond, and the Queen stretching out her hand took him out of the water. She placed him in the bed of pearl and began to nurse him, for the Sun, who never wears out, never grows old, is a baby from everlasting to everlasting. The woman came out from her concealment and taking a bottle of water from the pond, quickly retraced her steps. She arrived safely at her home, and sprinkled the water upon her son, who was healed. The report of this most wonderful journey of the woman was published all over the world, and princes and philosophers came from distant countries and from the ends of the earth to see the woman and the Sun-child, and to hear of all these wonderful things.

Among those who came from distant lands was the Dragon-child. He had returned safe from the wars and was surprised to find his bride changed, although the two step-sisters very much resembled one another. But as the Dragon-child had put a golden tooth in the place of the front tooth of his bride, which was broken in the well, he was able to detect the substitution. Upon a strict examination of his mother, he discovered that the bride had been sent to her stepmother's where, as he supposed, she had been gotten rid of, and was replaced by her stepsister. All his efforts to find his lost bride being in vain, the Dragon-child had come to see the Sun-child and his mother, with the expectation of finding some means for the discovery of his wife. He became a guest in the Sun-child's house, and told his story while they were eating supper. The bride, who was serving at the table, smiled and showed her golden tooth. This caused her to be discovered, and the Sun-child told how she had come and found him.

Now as they had partaken of bread together, they had become friends, and agreed to solve the difficulty in a friendly manner. They decided to roast salt meat and make the bride eat it, without letting her drink. Each was to take a pitcher of water, and they all were to go riding in the fields. He whom she should ask for a drink must be her husband. They did so, and took a ride in the fields, the wife accompanying them with her child in her arms. She was thirsty, but not wishing to offend any one of them, she kept silent for a time. Finally she saw that she would faint and must put an end to the perplexed state.

"Sun-child! Sun-child!" she exclaimed.

The Sun-child dismounted and prepared to give her a drink.

Thereupon she exclaimed, "Dragon-child! Dragon-child!"

He also dismounted and prepared to give her a drink.

Turning to the Sun-child, she said, "Here, take this child whose father you are, but I am the wedded wife of the Dragon-child."

And she drank from the Dragon-child's pitcher, and went home with him.

Thus their trouble ended and they attained their wishes. May all who are afflicted find consolation.

Abi Fressah's Feast

This story has been adapted from Gertrude Landa's version of the same tale that originally appeared in Jewish Fairy Tales and Legends, published in 1943 by Bloch Publishing Co. Inc., New York.

There was not in the whole city of Baghdad a greedier man than Abi Fressah, and you may be sure he was not popular. It was not that he was rich and refused to give heed to the needs of the poor. He was, in truth, a merchant in moderately affluent circumstances, and he did not withhold charity from the deserving, but he was a man of enormous appetite and did not scruple to descend to trickery to secure an invitation to a meal.

So skilful, indeed, did he become in wheedling these favours from his friends and from those with whom he traded, that he devoted the major portion of each day to feeding and left himself little time to attend to his business affairs. Moreover, he grew unpleasantly fat. His face was red and bloated with much wine drinking. He was not a nice person to look upon at all, and those who had once been his friends came to the conclusion that the day had arrived when he should be taught a severe lesson.

And so it came to pass that when Abi Fressah was standing in the bazaar at the hour of the mid-day meal and eagerly scanning the crowd to discover some acquaintance whom he could induce to ask him to dinner, he saw Ben Maslia, one of the wealthiest and most generous of men in Baghdad.

"Ah, my excellent friend," Abi cried, warmly greeting Ben Maslia, "'tis almost an eternity since my unworthy eyes were cast upon your pleasant countenance. Peace be on you and yours to the end of days."

"Also to you," returned Ben Maslia.

"And where have you come from? And where are you going, oh most hospitable friend?" Abi Fressah asked these questions hastily, his beady eyes searching the other's face hungrily for a sign upon which he could seize to invite himself to a meal. "It is the hour of the mid-day meal. Are you going, perchance, to your pious home?"

"Yes, I am going there," said Ben Maslia.

"My path lies in the same direction," said Abi Fressah. "It will be pleasant to walk together. Come," and he grasped Ben Maslia by the arm.

"It is kind of you, friend Abi Fressah," rejoined the other, "but I have built a new abode on the other side of the city."

Abi Fressah's face fell for a moment, but he was clever enough to take advantage of the news.

"A new dwelling erected by the wealthy Ben Maslia," he said, winningly, "must be a building of magnificence, worth seeing."

"Indeed it is as you say," cried the other enthusiastically, and forthwith he launched into a lavish description of his residence.

Abi Fressah grew impatient when Ben Maslia began to describe each room in detail, his hunger increased when, in glowing words, his friend painted the gorgeous dining-room, and his mouth watered at the information that the cellars were stocked with a thousand bottles of wine.

"Blessings on you and your wine-cellar and your house," murmured Abi Fressah, when he could get in a word. "I have no business of consequence to transact this afternoon. I could not pay you a better compliment than to spend it examining your treasures."

"Of a certainty you could not," assented the other, to his great glee.

"Then let us proceed," said Abi Fressah.

So they set out, Ben Maslia still continuing his glowing account of his wonderful house.

"It must be as spacious as a palace," put in Abi Fressah.

"You speak truth," agreed Ben Maslia. "I will illustrate to you the vast expanse of my new residence."

He stopped in his walk, measured one hundred paces in the street, and intimated that this represented the width of the central courtyard.

Abi Fressah was overwhelmed with surprise, but he was growing momentarily hungrier, and it was with difficulty he could restrain his impatience.

"Yes, yes," he said, "I would love to gaze upon the outer door of your dwelling."

"Such an outer door," said Ben Maslia, "have you never seen. Its width...." and again he began to measure the street to indicate its dimensions.

"And further," he added, calmly, either failing to notice, or deliberately overlooking Abi Fressah's growing distress, "its shape and design are...!" and he dragged the other through several streets until he found a door to which he could point as being not altogether unlike his own.

"But I weary you," he said, suddenly, as if regretful of the time he had wasted.

"No, no, not at all," Abi Fressah assured him, although he was inwardly fuming at the delay. "Your descriptions delight me immeasurably. You have not yet unfolded to me the wonders of your dining-room."

Thereupon Ben Maslia took up the tale of the dining-room and its furniture, and he dragged his companion half a mile out of their path to show him the furniture emporium where he had purchased the tables and the couches. Then he retraced his steps to point out a building from which he had borrowed certain ideas of decoration.

Abi Fressah's fat body was unused to such exertion. He perspired freely, his legs tottered beneath him, and his tongue was parched. He was really very uncomfortable, and the pangs of hunger from which he suffered were not lessened when Ben Maslia stopped outside a restaurant to speak to a friend who was just going in.

The conversation was prolonged, and all the time Abi Fressah's nose was tickled by the smell of the cooking. He endured agonies, especially when the friend invited Ben Maslia to dine with him, and Ben Maslia, after a few moment's hesitation, firmly declined.

"I must apologize to you for this delay," said Ben Maslia, when at length he left his friend, "but the matter was urgent. I will make up to you by the magnificence of the feast."

Abi Fressah thanked him cordially for his consideration, but his pain was intense when Ben Maslia insisted on giving him fullest particulars of all the dishes he would enjoy.

"Yes, yes," Abi kept saying, but Ben Maslia stayed his interruptions.

"Your dwelling is far from the centre of the city," Abi Fressah managed to say at last.

"That is a virtue," commented Ben Maslia, and he followed it up with the advice given to him by a renowned physician that a house was healthiest when it stood alone, away from the busy haunts of men. To all this and more, Abi Fressah was compelled to listen. His whole fat body ached with weariness, he was tortured by a raging thirst, and he fancied he felt himself growing thinner, so fearfully hungry was he.

The sun was sinking when at last they reached the house, and Abi Fressah was afraid for a moment that his host would enlarge upon its architecture. To his relief, however, they entered straightway, and Ben Maslia said to him, "You must be fatigued after your walk. Rest awhile."

Abi Fressah was truly grateful, and taking off his shoes he stretched himself on a comfortable couch. He dozed for a while, but was awakened by the noise of clattering dishes and the smell of savory cooking. He almost forgot his unpleasant afternoon in the prospect of the coming feast, but Ben Maslia did not appear. Abi Fressah soon felt angry. He could not restrain himself from banging a big brass gong to summon a servant. But although he banged several times, no servant answered the call. Abi Fressah nearly shed tears in his despair.

Suddenly Ben Maslia appeared before him.

"I thought I would give you ample rest," he said suavely. "Come, we must perform our ablutions."

Abi Fressah would have preferred to have dispensed with this ceremony, but he could not offend his host by declining to conform to the custom of the period. Ben Maslia led the way to the bath-chamber, and there they spent quite an hour. Then, thoroughly refreshed, the host said, "Now I will show you the wonders and beauties of my domain."

Abi Fressah was almost stupefied with hunger, but he had to permit himself to be led through each room and to hear again the praises that had already been poured into his ears all the afternoon. Only the smell of the cooking fortified his spirit and enabled him to undergo the ordeal. He seemed to wake up from a stupor when his host opened a door and exclaimed, "This is the feasting-chamber."

A scene of splendour burst upon the eyes of Abi Fressah. He rubbed his hands in glee and was ready to forget and forgive the discomforts of the past few hours. The dining-room presented a magnificent appearance, with its gorgeous hangings, its many lamps, and its marble floor. But these things Abi Fressah scarcely noted. His gaze was promptly directed on the table.

It was spread with the most sumptuous repast that ever he had seen. There were dishes upon dishes of tasty sweetmeats, huge platters of luscious fruits, many bottles of wine, and covered bowls from which arose the most appetizing aroma. Abi Fressah's mouth began to twitch and his eyes glowed. He moved forward to a seat.

"Good friend," said his host, "let me first introduce to your notice my staff of servants."

He clapped his hands, and immediately, in quite startling fashion, a dozen servants stepped from behind the hangings which had hidden them and bowed before their master. With a dozen attendants to wait upon him, Abi Fressah saw that he was going to enjoy a meal worthy of the occasion. He looked upon the slaves with satisfaction.

"Note, my worthy Abi Fressah," said Ben Maslia, "that this is no ordinary retinue of servants. Each one comes from a different part of the known world. Rosh, the big man there, head of them all, is the only native of Baghdad. He has an interesting history. He has been in my service since his birth. His father was likewise in the service of my sainted father, and his grandfather.... But let that suffice. I would not imprison your appetite longer. Sheni, that is the second servant, bring us the first dish."

Sheni took up one of the dishes from the table and placed himself by the side of his master.

"He stands well, doesn't he?" asked Ben Maslia, in admiring tones. "He is a descendant of kings. In ancient days his ancestors sat on a throne and ruled over a huge territory beyond the deserts of Africa. I obtained him during my journey in that country. And on that occasion I discovered this beautiful rug in a shop in Cairo."

Saying which, Ben Maslia rose from his seat and fingered lovingly one of the hangings of the room. Abi Fressah did not rise. He was trying to keep his temper. The dish which Sheni held so tantalizingly under his very nose made him mad with hunger and desire.

But Ben Maslia took no heed. He began to dilate upon the virtues of another piece of tapestry.

"This," he said, "I bought in the famous bazaar of Damascus. It is hundreds of years old. And in that city, too, I became possessed of my third servant, Shelishi there, a true-born son of the Holy Land and the keeper of my camels. Our meeting was an adventure...."

Abi Fressah was not listening. This was beyond endurance. He felt that soon he would collapse in a faint on the floor. And still Ben Maslia droned on. There was a servant from China and also a cunningly wrought vase from that land. There was a brown page boy in a red turban from India from which land his host had also brought the lamp standing in the centre of the table and some of the flowers which adorned the room.

"You would not guess," he was saying, "that many of these blooms are not natural. They are artificial but mixed so skilfully with the real that even experts would be deluded."

By this time Abi Fressah was beyond the power of speech. Two or three times, he tried to speak but could not. He was really too weak. Never in his life before had he been so hungry, so tortured. It was some time, however, before Ben Maslia noticed his plight.

"Are you ill?" he exclaimed. "That grieves me. But, fortunately, I have in the house an experienced apothecary who can apply leeches and relieve you of foul blood."

"No, no," pleaded the unhappy Abi Fressah, finding his tongue at this dismal prospect.

"Perchance a glass of rare cordial will revive you," said Ben Maslia, taking one of the bottles from the table.

Abi Fressah managed to gasp the word "Yes," and Rosh held a goblet into which Ben Maslia poured a rich, red fluid.

"Drink this," he said kindly, holding the cup to his guest's lip.

"At last," thought Abi Fressah, as he opened his mouth.

The next moment he sprang from his stool with astonishing agility, spluttering and cursing. The liquid was bitter in the extreme, the taste it left in his mouth most horrid.

"Now I know I have been hoodwinked," he screamed in rage, and he dashed toward the outer door.

"Stay, stay, whatever is the matter?" cried Ben Maslia.

"Stop, stop," echoed the servants, as Abi Fressah commenced to run.

The cry was taken up in the street by those who saw a fat man panting along in the darkness, pursued by a number of servants.

"Stop thief!" was the cry of one man in his excitement. The town guards heard, and without any ado they seized Abi Fressah and hauled him off to the jail. In vain he begged for mercy and struggled for freedom.

"If you will not behave, we shall use force," the guards said, and they beat him with staves.

At the jail, Abi Fressah was flung into a cell, and there, on a bed of straw on the ground, he spent a horrible, sleepless night. He ached in every bone in his body, he was bruised all over, and his hunger was such that he felt he had never eaten in his life. His reflections were sad, as you may well imagine, and they led him to a vow that never again would he seek the hospitality of his friends. He realized at last that he had made himself obnoxious and had been cleverly and deservedly well punished.

Even yet his sufferings were not at an end, for next morning, when he was released and sent for his physician, the latter prescribed a diet of gruel and barley water for a whole week!

Legends Of Artasches And Artavasd

This story has been adapted from Louis A. Boettiger's version of the same tale that originally appeared in Armenian Legends and Festivals, published in 1920 by University of Minnesota, Minneapolis.

The legends of Artasches and Satenik, and of Artavasd, the son of Artasches, belong to the Arsacid period, for Artavasd and Artasches are Armenian kings of the Arsacid dynasty, according to Moses.

The Alans who, according to the legend, were a neighboring people residing in the mountain region in the vicinity of Georgia, spread themselves over Armenia while Artasches, the Armenian king, collected a great army and forced the Alans to retreat across the river Kur where they pitched camp.

The son of the Alan king was taken captive and brought to Artasches, which forced the former to seek peace on whatever terms the Armenian king might wish, provided only his son was returned in safety. But Artasches refused, whereupon the sister of the captured boy came to the riverbank, and standing upon a great rock spoke to the men in the camp of Artasches by means of interpreters saying, "Oh brave Artasches, who has vanquished the great nation of Alans, I speak to you. Come, listen to the bright-eyed daughter of the Alan king and give back the boy. For it is not the way of heroes to destroy life at the root, nor for the sake of humbling and enslaving a hostage to establish everlasting enmity between two great nations."

Artasches, having heard these words went to the riverbank and having seen that the girl was beautiful, and having listened to her words of wisdom, wished to marry her. His chamberlain considered it a wise stroke of policy, and therefore went to the Alan king, soliciting the hand of the princess for his master, whose oaths and assurances of peace he vouched for, together with the promise to return the boy.

The king of the Alans answered, "From where shall brave Artasches give thousands upon thousands, and ten thousands upon tens of thousands in return for the maiden?"

Brave king Artasches mounted his fine black charger, and took much gold, leather, and crimson dye with him as a dowry. Like a swift winged eagle he passed over the river and, having paid the bride price, he cast a golden ring round the waist of the Alan princess, causing much pain to the tender maiden as he bore her swiftly back to his camp.

It rained showers of gold when Artasches became a bridegroom, It rained pearls when Princess Satenik became a bride. For it was the custom of kings to scatter coins amongst the people when they arrived at the doors of the temple for their wedding, as also for the queens to scatter pearls in their bride-chamber.

After fifty-one years of a very prosperous reign, Artasches, who was very much beloved by his people, died. The funeral procession was a most magnificent one, and many of the people killed themselves, out of love for their dead king, according to the custom of the time. And when the body was laid in the grave they threw precious jewels, gold, and silver after it. Nor did the lamenting and suicide stop after his burial, for upon the grave of their dead king the nobles and the people continued to kill themselves. So great was the slaughter that Artavasd, son of Artasches, and king after his father's death, addressed the spirit of his dead father, saying, "Behold, you are taking all with you. Will you leave me to rule over ruins and the dead?"

Whereupon the spirit of Artasches cursed him and said, "When you ride forth to hunt over the free heights of Ararat, the strong ones shall have you, and shall take you up on to the free heights of Ararat. There shall you abide, and never more see the light."

It came to pass that one day while out hunting Artavasd was seized by some visionary terror and lost his reason. Urging his horse down a steep bank he fell into a chasm where he sank and disappeared. Old women told how he was confined in a cavern and bound with iron chains which his two dogs gnawed at daily in order to set him free. But somehow at the sound of the hammers striking on the anvils, the chains were continually strengthened. Artavasd spent his remaining years alone in the solitude of Ararat in accordance with his father's curse.

Bedik And The Invulnerable Giant

This story has been adapted from Abraham G. Seklemian's version of the same tale that originally appeared in The Golden Maiden and Other Folk Tales and Fairy Stories Told in Armenia, published in 1898 by The Helman-Taylor Company, New York. This tale is based on earlier work undertaken by Ohannes Chatschumian, who, before his death, had begun a compilation of 'Armenian' folklore for Miss Alice Fletcher. These 'Armenian' tales themselves originated in the Byzantine peasant tradition that developed over the preceding fifteen hundred years.

Many years ago there was a King who had seven sons. As soon as each one of the princes was of age his father sent him on an expedition, so that he might display his bravery and marry the maiden whom he preferred. Thus six of the princes acquired wives, but Heaven only knows whether they displayed real bravery or not.

It was now the turn of the seventh son, whose name was Bedik. His father gave him a horse of lightning, a magic sword and a bow-and-arrow, saying, "Go, my son, and may Heaven grant you good luck."

Bedik started and travelled through the length and breadth of the world, visiting the land of darkness, the land of light, the land of fairies, the land of giants. He did battle with men, beasts, genii, and all kinds of creatures which he encountered on the way, and overcame them all, but in his wars he lost all his servants and his wealth. He was alone, one day, when he came to a magnificent castle built of marble, decorated with gold and jewels and surrounded with orchards and flower gardens. He walked about the building and gazed everywhere, but could see no human being, man or woman. He waited all day, concealed behind some bushes. Toward evening there came a Giant covered all over with armour, brandishing his bow and arrows, which were of heavy steel. When he walked the earth trembled. When he came near the castle, becoming aware of the presence of a human being, he exclaimed, "Aha! I smell a human being. I go hunting in the mountains, and the prey has come to my home. Ho! Human being, disclose yourself, or else I will make a morsel of you."

The lad was looking at the Giant from his place of concealment. He was the strangest creature that he had ever seen. Neither a sword nor an arrow could pierce him. Nevertheless he decided to face him, and coming out from behind the bushes, the lad stood before him.

"Who are you?" asked the Giant. "The bird with its wing, and the snake on its belly could not approach this castle of mine, so how could you venture to come? Have you not heard of the fame of the Invulnerable Giant?"

"I have," said the lad bravely, "and my name is no less famous than yours. I am Bedik. I have travelled all over the world, and having heard of you, I came to measure swords with you."

The Giant gazed at the lad for a moment and suddenly sneezed. The burst of air through his nostrils caused the lad to leap ten rods away.

"Hello!" exclaimed the Giant, laughing, "you do not seem to be very well able to fight me, do you? No, come here again;. Do not be afraid, I will not hurt you. I have heard about you, and you are a brave little fellow. But you see you can do no harm to me because I am invulnerable. Come, be my servant, for I need a skilful human servant, and I do not think I can find a better one than you. Bring your sword and bow and arrows. You know that they cannot pierce me, but we may need them for hunting and other purposes."

The lad consented, and they lived together for a time. One day the Giant said to the youth, "You see I am immortal, but I have an anxiety which gnaws my heart day and night. The King of the East has a daughter, and there is no beauty like hers under the sun. I have made seven expeditions to carry her away, but so far have not succeeded. If you can bring her here I will bestow upon you a kingly reward."

"I will bring her for you," said the lad.

"But do you promise it upon your soul?" said the Giant.

"I do," answered the lad, and at once started on the expedition.

After a long journey he came to the city of the King of the East, changed his clothes, took the shape of a farmer boy, and became the apprentice of the King's gardener. He saw the King's daughter sitting in her window and working with her needle. She was so beautiful that she seemed to say to the sun, "Sun, you need not shine, since I am shining." The lad fell in love with her and began to curse the hour when he made the solemn promise to convey her to the Giant.

One day, taking advantage of the absence of his master, the lad stripped off his humble clothes, and putting on his princely garments, mounted his horse of lightning and rode in the King's garden. The maiden was looking from her window and saw him. She had never seen a young man so perfect, and she fell in love with him.

On the following day she sent two of her maids to the youth, informing him of her love. The lad sent her word of who he was, how he had heard of her wondrous beauty, and now he was waiting to do anything that she might order. The city was surrounded by high walls, through fear of the Invulnerable Giant, who assaulted it every year with the intention of carrying off the maiden, but the people of the city, being brave fighters, would not let the maiden be borne away. So the lad had a hard task to perform. One day the girl sent to him, through her maids, the following message:

"To-morrow is the feast of the Navasard, when all the maidens of the city go out for recreation and merriment, but I am not allowed to go forth because it is the day when the Invulnerable Giant makes his annual assault to seize me. I will, however, go to the garden by the riverside, which is surrounded by high walls; there I will wait for you to see you display your bravery."

Having received this message, on the next day the youth put on his princely garments, girded his magic sword, and taking his bow and arrows, mounted his horse of lightning. Once or twice he coursed the steed near the garden wall, until it began to gallop as fast as if it had wings. One stroke of the whip, and it jumped over the wall like an eagle, and instantly the horse and its rider alighted in the middle of the garden. In the twinkling of an eye the lad put his arm around the maiden's waist, and placing her behind him on the saddle, gave another stroke of the whip, which made the horse leap over the garden wall, and in a second they were on safe ground outside the city galloping like a flash of lightning.

The maids in attendance were horror-stricken, thinking that it was a hurricane which had taken their lady from them. It was a long time before they understood what had taken place, but then they informed the King, who sent out his bravest horsemen in pursuit of the fugitives. But it was too late. The couple on the back of the horse of lightning passed over the mountains and valleys until they came to the border of the deep river. A stroke of the whip and the steed swam the deep waters and emerged on the other side. The King's horsemen came as far as the river, but seeing that the couple had crossed the frontier, they returned.

As soon as the maiden and the youth had crossed the water, and the Invulnerable Giant's castle appeared in the distance, the maiden said to the lad, "Bedik, dearest, we have come so far and you have not yet spoken a single word to me. You have shown no sign of love. For Heaven's sake, tell me, did you kidnap me for yourself or for another?"

"You said, 'for Heaven's sake,'" replied the lad, "I will, therefore, tell you the truth. I have kidnaped you for the Invulnerable Giant. I have promised to deliver you to him."

"Alas!" exclaimed the maiden. "May Heaven's curse rest upon the Invulnerable! He could not get me for all the world. You do not reflect that it was by your skill and valour that you secured me. Woe to frail womanhood! Maidens are the slaves of their hearts. For you, only for you, I eloped. If you reject me, here is the deep water, and here the high precipice. I would better be food for fishes and birds. May Heaven's fire burn and consume the hard hearts of men!"

So saying, she prepared to throw herself down the abyss into the deep water. The lad's heart began to burn like a furnace, and he took hold of her, crying, "No, dearest, do not harm yourself. It was because of the vow I made upon my soul that I am taking you to the Giant, and the day you become his wife I will put an end to my life with this sword, for without you, life for me would be a curse."

Then they exchanged vows that they would use every means to put a speedy end to the Invulnerable Giant, and then be married; because they could not marry without destroying the Giant. Thereupon, they mounted the horse and began to proceed toward the castle. The Giant, who from the tower of the castle was looking their way, seeing them at a distance, immediately came down and ran to meet them. He expressed his gratitude to the lad, and his excess of love to the maiden. He treated her with extreme kindness, fearing that he might hurt her tender feelings with his unpolished manners.

"Are you pleased with this place?" he asked her. "What do you want me to do in order to make you as happy as possible?"

"I am very well, thank you. You are everything for me," said the maiden, suppressing her bitter hatred towards him. "But my parents consented to send me to you only under the condition that I should keep myself a virgin seven years longer. I have given an oath that I will do so, otherwise the love with which they have cherished me would turn into poison and defile my whole life. Do you accept this condition?"

"I do," said the Giant. "As you are now in my hand, I am willing to wait not only seven years, but, if necessary, seven times seven years."

They exchanged solemn vows, and decided that Bedik should live with them, and be the best man at their wedding. The maiden occupied one apartment of the castle, the youth and the Giant the other apartments, and so they lived for a time. But the lad and the maiden were uneasy. It was in vain to think of killing the Giant, for he was invulnerable. If they eloped he would certainly overtake them, and there was no escaping from his wrath.

One day as the Giant was lying on the couch, with his head on the maiden's lap, she said to him, "In former times, how did you live alone, without any companions? And how is it that you are invulnerable, when so many arrows and swords are thrown at you? What is the secret of your immortality?"

At first the Giant refused to tell, but the maiden importuned him, saying, "If you will not inform me, then you do not love me. Tell me in plain words that you love me not, and I will cease to live."

The Giant was at last persuaded to give up his secret, and he said, "Seven days' journey from this castle there is a white mountain, where lives an unsubduable white bull which neither man nor beast dares to approach. Once in seven days he becomes thirsty and goes to the top of the white mountain, where there is a white fountain with seven white marble reservoirs full of water, which he drains at a single draught. The bull has in his belly a white fox, which in its turn has in its belly a white box made of mother-of-pearl. In that box are seven white sparrows. Those are my spirits, and those are my seven secrets. The bull cannot be subdued, the fox cannot be caught, the box cannot be opened, the sparrows cannot be seized. If either of them is taken, the others will escape. So I remain unconquerable and invulnerable and immortal."

The maiden told the secret to Bedik, adding, "I have done what I could, but now it remains for you to do the rest."

After a few days the lad girded on his sword, and bearing his bow and arrow, took leave of the Giant, saying that he would go on a month's journey. He started and went directly to the convent of the seven wise monks, who were renowned all over the world for their great erudition and learning. After performing his religious duties before the holy altar, he asked the monks, "How is the unconquerable man conquered, and the unsubduable beast subdued?"

And he received the following answer, "Man by woman; beast by wine."

On the following day he loaded seven horses with seven skinfuls of seven-year-old wine and took them to the white mountain. He emptied the water out of the seven marble reservoirs and filled them with wine, turning the water of the fountain elsewhere. Nearby he dug a trench, and hiding himself, waited for the result. At the end of seven days the white bull came to drink, and smelling the wine, he was so much terrified that he leaped as high as the height of seven poplar trees, and ran back roaring and bellowing. On the following day he returned, and being thirsty, drank the wine and was overcome. He leaped once or twice and fell down senseless. The lad drew his sword and approached and cut off the bull's head.

Let us return a moment to the palace of the Giant. It was the last day of the seven years during which he had waited for the maiden. He had gone to the hunt, that they might have noble game for their wedding dinner. When the bull was overcome and fell, the giant began to grow drowsy. As soon as the youth cut off the bull's head, the Giant turned dizzy, and a tremor ran through his frame.

"Alas!" cried the Giant. "Someone has killed the white bull. I know it is my fault. I gave my secret to the maiden, and she has told it to Bedik or to some other lover. The bull is killed, and I must die. I will go and kill the maiden. She is not to be for me, so why shall she be for another?" So saying, he began to run toward the castle.

Bedik cut the bull's belly open. The fox also was drunk and stupid, and he cut off his head. The Giant lost his senses, and the blood began to gush out of his nostrils. The youth, opening the stomach of the fox, obtained the pearl box and put it in warm blood. The lid was opened, and the lad seized the seven sparrows. Thereupon streams of blood began to run from the Giant's mouth and ears, and his two eye-balls started from their sockets, like two great pomegranates. But still he was running toward the castle, sword in hand, and roaring like a mad beast. The maiden was horror-stricken, and quickly ran up to the top of the tower, determined to throw herself there and kill herself, rather than fall into the hands of the Giant.

The Giant had barely reached the castle door, when Bedik killed two of the sparrows. With that the two knees of the Giant were broken. He killed two more sparrows, and the Giant's two arms withered. He killed two more, and the lungs and heart of the Giant ceased to breathe and beat. He killed the last sparrow. The Giant knocked his head against the threshold of the castle, his skull was broken, and his brains oozed out. A black smoke rose from his mouth and nostrils, and he lay dead as a stone. Thereupon Bedik came on horseback like a flash of lightning. The maiden descended from the tower, and they embraced one another. At once they decided to go to the maiden's parents and celebrate their wedding. They collected all the wealth of the Invulnerable Giant, and mounting the horse of lightning, began to proceed toward the East.

The King of the East grieved sorely because the maiden was his only child. Seeing that he was getting old, and there was no successor to his throne made him deeply saddened. On the day following the maiden's disappearance, the King had sent his servants to the seven wise monks, asking their advice, and he had received the following message, "The hero who carried off your daughter is a Prince. At the end of seven years your daughter will be restored to you by the same hero, as pure and chaste as before."

The anxious father waited for seven long years. It was the last day of the seventh year. The King and his subjects had made great preparations for the reception of the returning Princess and her hero. Towards evening the King and his peers were looking anxiously from the seven towers of the city wall. The sun was just going down, when a flash as of lightning was seen on the western horizon, and in the twinkling of an eye Bedik and the maiden reached the city gate on the back of their fiery steed. They were received amid the wild acclamations of the crowd, and were led to the King's palace. There they knelt before the King and told their story. The King blessed them, and for forty days and forty nights the wedding feast was celebrated.

They attained their wish. May Heaven grant that you may attain your wishes!

The Beggar King

This story has been adapted from Gertrude Landa's version of the same tale that originally appeared in Jewish Fairy Tales and Legends, published in 1943 by Bloch Publishing Co. Inc., New York.

Proud King Hagag sat on his throne in state, and the high priest, standing by his side, read from the Holy Book, as was his daily custom. He read these words, "For riches are not for ever, and the crown does not endure through every generation?"

"Cease!" cried the king. "Who wrote those words?"

"They are the words of the Holy Book," answered the high priest.

"Give me the book," commanded the king.

With trembling hands the high priest placed it before his majesty. King Hagag gazed earnestly at the words that had been read, and he frowned. Raising his hand, he tore the page from the book and threw it to the ground.

"I, Hagag, am king," he said, "and all such passages that offend me shall be torn out."

He flung the volume angrily from him while the high priest and all his courtiers looked on in astonishment.

"I have heard enough for today," he said. "Too long have I delayed my hunting expedition. Get the horses ready."

He descended from the throne, stalked haughtily past the trembling figure of the high priest, and went off to the hunt. Soon he was riding furiously across an open plain toward a forest where a wild stag had been seen. A trumpet sounded the signal that the deer had been driven from its hiding place, and the king urged his horse forward to be the first in the chase. His majesty's steed was the swiftest in the land. Quickly it carried him out of sight of his nobles and attendants. But the deer was surprisingly fleet and the king could not catch up with it. Coming to a river, the animal plunged in and swam across. Scrambling up the opposite bank its antlers caught in the branch of a tree, and the king, arriving at the river, gave a cry of joy.

"Now I have you," he said. Springing from his horse and divesting himself of his clothing he swam across with nothing but a sword.

As he reached the opposite bank, however, the deer freed itself from the tree and plunged into a thicket. The king, with his sword in his hand, followed quickly, but he could not find the deer. Instead, he found, lying on the ground beyond the thicket, a beautiful youth clad in a deer-skin. He was panting as if after a long run. The king stood still in surprise and the youth sprang to his feet.

"I am the deer," he said. "I am a genii and I have lured you to this spot, proud king, to teach you a lesson for your words this morning."

Before King Hagag could recover from his surprise the youth ran back to the river and swam across. Quickly he dressed himself in the king's clothes and mounted the horse just as the other hunters came up. They thought the genii was King Hagag and they halted before him.

"Let us return," said the genii. "The deer has crossed the river and has escaped."

King Hagag from the thicket on the opposite side watched them ride away and then flung himself on the ground and wept bitterly. There he lay until a wood-cutter found him.

"What are you doing here?" asked the man.

"I am King Hagag," returned the monarch.

"You are a fool," said the wood-cutter. "You are a lazy good-for-nothing to talk so. Come, carry my bundle of sticks and I will give you food and an old garment."

In vain the king protested. The wood-cutter only laughed the more, and at last, losing patience, he beat him and drove him away. Tired and hungry, and clad only in the rags which the wood-cutter had given him, King Hagag reached the palace late at night.

"I am King Hagag," he said to the guards, but roughly they told him to go away, and after spending a wretched night in the streets of the city, his majesty, next morning, was glad to accept some bread and milk offered to him by a poor old woman who took pity on him. He stood at a street corner not knowing what to do. Little children teased him; others took him for a beggar and offered him money. Later in the day he saw the genii ride through the streets on his horse. All the people bowed down before him and cried, "Long live the king!"

"Woe is me," cried Hagag, in his wretchedness. "I am punished for my sin in scoffing at the words of the Holy Book."

He saw that it would be useless for him to go to the palace again, and he went into the fields and tried to earn his bread as a labourer. He was not used to work, however, and but for the kindness of the very poorest he would have died of starvation. He wandered miserably from place to place until he fell in with some blind beggars who had been deserted by their guide. Joyfully he accepted their offer to take the guide's place.

Months rolled by, and one morning the royal heralds went forth and announced that "Good King Hagag" would give a feast a week from that day to all the beggars in the land.

From far and near came beggars in hundreds, to partake of the king's bounty, and Hagag stood among them, with his blind companions, in the courtyard of the palace waiting for his majesty to appear. He knew the place well, and he hung his head and wept.

"His majesty will speak to each one of you who are his guests today," cried a herald, and one by one they passed into the palace and stood before the throne. When it came to Hagag's turn, he trembled so much that he had to be supported by the guards.

The genii on the throne and Hagag looked at each other for a long time.

"Are you, too, a beggar?" said the genii.

"No, gracious majesty," answered Hagag with bent head. "I have sinned grievously and have been punished. I am but the servant of a troop of blind beggars to whom I act as guide."

The genii king signed to his courtiers that he desired to be left alone with Hagag. Then he said, "Hagag, I know you. I see that you have repented. It is well. Now you can resume your rightful place."

"Gracious majesty," said Hagag, "I have learned humility and wisdom. The throne is not for me. The blind beggars need me. Let me remain in their service."

"It cannot be," said the genii. "I see that you are truly penitent. Your lesson is learned and my task is done. I will see that the blind beggars are well taken care of."

With his own hands he placed the royal robes on Hagag and himself donned those of the beggar. When the courtiers returned they saw no difference. King Hagag sat on the throne again, and nowhere in the whole world was there a monarch who ruled more wisely or showed more kindness and sympathy to all his subjects.

Simon, The Friend Of Snakes

This story has been adapted from Abraham G. Seklemian's version of the same tale that originally appeared in The Golden Maiden and Other Folk Tales and Fairy Stories Told in Armenia, published in 1898 by The Helman-Taylor Company, New York. This tale is based on earlier work undertaken by Ohannes Chatschumian, who, before his death, had begun a compilation of 'Armenian' folklore for Miss Alice Fletcher. These 'Armenian' tales themselves originated in the Byzantine peasant tradition that developed over the preceding fifteen hundred years.

The King of the Snakes lives in the ruins of a big tower between Nineveh and Babylon, and rules all the snake tribe, both on land and sea. Once the King's son, who was viceroy of the province of Diarbekir, wrote a letter to his royal father, as follows:

"Long live the King! May Heaven bestow upon you life everlasting. Amen. Be it known to you that your daughter-in-law and grandchildren were sick last summer, and the doctors advised that they must have a change of climate and must go to Mount Ararat and bathe in its pure streams, and eat its fragrant flowers, and this will immediately heal them. Consequently I sent her and the children, with their attendants, to Mount Ararat. I also wrote letters

to the provincial viceroys and princes to assist the Princess and her train during their sojourn in that district. But the Prince of Aderbadagan, after receiving my letter, instead of giving help to the traveling Princess, collected his troops and assaulted her and her train. The attendants of the Princess met them bravely, and there, at the foot of Mount Ararat, occurred a bloody battle, which would doubtless have resulted in the total defeat of the Princess' train, on account of the superior numbers of the enemy, if a human being, Simon the Shepherd, who was tending his flock in a neighboring field, had not come to the assistance of our fatigued combatants. He took his great club, and entering the ranks of the warriors, beat and killed and pursued the assaulting brigands of the Prince of Aderbadagan, and saved the life of your daughter-in-law, who thus came safely through this perilous journey. You see, my liege, that there is good even among men. I will punish the vile Prince of Aderbadagan for his wicked conduct; but it remains for you to reward the goodness of this noble human being as you deem best, and oblige your affectionate son."

The King of the Snakes, receiving this letter, took with him a vast quantity of gold and jewels, and went to his palace, in a ruined castle between Aleppo and Diarbekir. He posted his attendants on the highways to keep watch and inform him when Shepherd Simon should pass. The Shepherd was employed by dealers in live-stock, who did business with Damascus and Aleppo, and was now on his way to Aleppo. As soon as he approached the palace of the Snake King the watchers informed their sovereign, and in the twinkling of an eye the whole army of snakes stood near the highway and began to conjure. Simon the Shepherd felt a strange dizziness, and the heavens above and the earth below seemed to change. He stood there bewitched, while his companions drove away. Presently he opened his eyes, and he was surrounded by innumerable snakes of all sizes and colours. Upon a golden throne was sitting a snake as thick as the body of an elephant, and upon his head there was a crown of costly jewels and diamonds. One of the snakes read a paper praising the goodness of the Shepherd, his natural fondness for the snake tribe, and his gallant defence of the weak and the wronged.

"Now, noble human being," said the King, "here is gold for you, and precious jewels and diamonds. Take as much as you like, and in addition to these, if you have a desire in your heart tell it to me and I will cause it to be satisfied."

Simon, after filling his shepherd's bag and his pockets with gold and jewels, said, "I wish to understand the language of all animals, reptiles and birds."

"Let it be so," said the King, "but the day on which you shall tell anything of what you have seen or heard, you shall die."

The spell was removed, the snakes vanished, and Simon the Shepherd returned to his home near the foot of Mount Ararat. On the way he heard the animals talking, and they knew all the secrets of men, and foretold events that would happen. Sometimes he laughed at what he heard, and sometimes he was terrified so that his hair stood erect upon his head. He entered his native village, and all the dogs, cats, chickens, and even the long-legged storks were hallooing to one another and saying, "Simon the Shepherd has come, and his bag and pockets are full of gold and jewels."

Simon came to his house and put his treasure before his wife who, being a very curious woman, instantly asked him where and how he obtained so much wealth.

"Enjoy it, but never ask," answered Simon.

Simon heard his dog and chickens talking in regard to the secrets of his house. Sometimes he laughed and sometimes he was angry. His wife, noticing Simon's strange conduct towards the animals, asked the reason. He refused to tell, but she begged and importuned him, weeping all the time. Finally he could resist her entreaties no longer, and he promised to tell her everything on the following day. That evening he heard the dog talking to the cock, which was leading the chickens to roost, chuckling and gurgling, "Tell me, master rooster," said the dog, "what is the use of your chuckling and gurgling, since our master has promised his wife tomorrow to tell her everything? He will die. People will come and kill you, shoot me, and plunder and ruin everything which belongs to our master."

"Hah! The sooner it is ruined the better," answered the rooster, contemptuously. "I have a family of forty wives, who are all obedient to me. If our master was as wise as he is rich, he would not pay attention to the vain inquisitiveness of his wife; he himself would not die, and no harm would befall us or his house. But now he deserves death."

Hearing this, Simon was advised. He seized his great club, and stood before his wife, saying, "Wife, you must stop trying to compel me to tell you the secret. Be content with what you have; else, by Heaven, I will beat you to death!"

The woman, seeing the club brandished over her head, put an end to her inquiries, and thereafter they enjoyed a happy life.

The Maiden Of The Sea

This story has been adapted from Abraham G. Seklemian's version of the same tale that originally appeared in The Golden Maiden and Other Folk Tales and Fairy Stories Told in Armenia, published in 1898 by The Helman-Taylor Company, New York. This tale is based on earlier work undertaken by Ohannes Chatschumian, who, before his death, had begun a compilation of 'Armenian' folklore for Miss Alice Fletcher. These 'Armenian' tales themselves originated in the Byzantine peasant tradition that developed over the preceding fifteen hundred years.

There was an old woman and her son who lived on the seacoast. She used to cast a loaf of bread into the sea every morning. One day she said to her son, "My son, I am getting old, and I feel that I shall soon die. Listen to my advice, and every morning cast a loaf of bread to the sea."

The old woman died, and the lad continued casting a loaf of bread into the sea every morning. One evening as he came back home from his work he was surprised to see the house swept and cleaned. Another day he put some meat in the cupboard, and in the evening, the meat was cooked and the table ready for him. This was repeated several times. One day he hid himself under the stairs. Soon a splash of water was heard in the sea, and, a big fish jumped to the house doorway. At once the skin of the fish fell down, and out of it came a maiden as beautiful as the shining moon. She swept the house clean, and finishing the kitchen work was just going out of the door, when the lad took hold of her.

"Mamma, mamma! Help me!" exclaimed the maiden. Immediately a voice came from the sea, "Don't be afraid, daughter, that is my son-in-law." By the will of God and the permission of the mother, the maiden became the bride of the lad. At once the priest was called, who performed the marriage ceremony, and for seven days they celebrated the wedding festival.

One day, as the bride was working with a needle before the window, the Prince, who was taking a walk in his seashore orchard, saw her and was enchanted by her beauty. Finding out that she was a married woman, he decided to destroy her husband and get her in marriage. He immediately summoned the lad, and said, "I want you to make me a tent so large that all my army may be accommodated in it, and yet half of it remain empty. I will give you three days' time to prepare it. If you don't make it ready by that time your head shall be cut off and all your property confiscated."

The lad came home with a sad face. What should he say to the Prince at the end of the third day? Surely his head should be cut off. His bride, seeing him, said, "How now, husband! What is the matter? Why are you sad today?"

"Nothing," answered the lad, sighing.

"No, your face is changed," said the bride. "I pray you what is the matter?"

The lad told her what the Prince had ordered him to do.

"Never mind, husband," said she, and putting her head out of the window toward the sea, she cried, "Mamma, mamma! Send us up our small tent, please. We want to go camping."

The small tent was thrown up from the sea. The lad took it to the Prince. It took his servants seven days to pitch it. Not only the Prince's army, but all his people were accommodated in it, and yet half of it was empty.

"This is right well," said the Prince, "but you see there is no furniture to put on the ground. I want you to bring me a rug to suit the tent exactly. If you don't bring it in three days your head shall be cut off."

The lad told his wife, and she asked her mother to send up the small rug, which was taken to the Prince. The Prince next day asked the lad to fetch him a cluster of grapes so large that all his army might eat and not be able to finish it. On the following day that also was brought. Then the Prince wanted him to bring him a three-day old baby who could walk and talk like grown-up people. This time the lad was dismayed, because it was a sheer impossibility, and he thought he would surely lose his head this time.

"Never mind that, husband," said his wife, in the evening, and turning toward the sea, she cried, "Mamma! Send the baby up here for a while, we want to see him."

The baby was given up, and the lad took him to the Prince, still doubting in his mind whether the baby could do what the Prince required. On the way the lad's foot slipped and the baby was shaken.

"Have you not your eyes about you, brother-in-law," the baby said, "or have you a mind to fall down and crush me under you?"

The lad was pleased at the baby's reproach because it assured him that his head would not be cut off. On being presented to the Prince the baby at once walked toward him, jumped up to his lap and giving the Prince a box on his ear, said, "Are you not ashamed, Prince, to give so much trouble to my brother-in-law? You want to kill him and be married to my sister, do you? For shame, Prince, for shame!"

Thereupon the Prince gave up his evil intention, apologized to the lad and asked forgiveness. So the lad and his bride of the sea were left unmolested and they are still living on the border of the sea.

The Quarrel Of The Cat And Dog

This story has been adapted from Gertrude Landa's version of the same tale that originally appeared in Jewish Fairy Tales and Legends, published in 1943 by Bloch Publishing Co. Inc., New York.

In the childhood of the world, when Adam named all the animals and ruled over them, the dog and the cat were the greatest good friends. They were inseparable chums in their recreations, faithful partners in their transactions, and devoted comrades in all their adventures, their pleasures and their sorrows. They lived together, shared each other's food and confided their secrets to none but themselves. It seemed that no possible difference would ever arise to cause trouble between them.

Then winter came. It was a new experience to them to feel the cold wind cutting through their skins and making them shiver. The dismal prospect of the leafless trees and the hard cold ground weighed heavily upon their hearts, and, worse still, there was less food. The scarcity grew serious, and hunger plunged them into unhappiness and despair. Doggie became melancholy, while Pussie grew peevish, then petulant, and finally developed a horrid temper.

"We can't go on like this," moaned the cat. "I think we had better dissolve our partnership. We can't find enough to share when we are together, but separately we ought each to discover sufficient forage in our hunting."

"I think I can help you, because I am the stronger," said the dog.

Pussie did not contradict her friend, but she thought the dog a bit of a fool and too good-natured. She knew herself to be sly and intended to rely on that quality for her future sustenance. Doggie was deeply hurt at Pussie's desire to end their happy compact, but he said quietly, "Of course, if you insist on parting, I will agree."

"It is agreed then," purred Pussie.

"Where will you go?" asked Doggie.

"To the house of Adam," promptly replied the cat, who had evidently made up her mind. "There are mice there. Adam will be grateful if I clear them away. I shall have food to eat."

"Very well," assented the dog. "I will wander further afield."

Then the cat said solemnly, "We must each take an oath never to cross the other's path. That is the proper way to terminate a business agreement. The serpent says so, and he is the wisest of all animals."

They put their right fore-paws together and gravely repeated an oath never to interfere with each other by going to the same place. Then they parted. Doggie trotted off sorrowfully with his head hanging down. Once he looked back, but Puss did not do so. She scampered off as fast as she could to the house of Adam.

"Father Adam," she cried, "I have come to be your slave. You are troubled with mice in the house. I can rid you of them, and I want nothing else for my services."

"You are welcome," said Father Adam, stroking Pussie's warm fur.

Puss rubbed her head against his feet, purred contentedly, and ran off to look for mice. She found plenty and soon grew fat and comfortable. Adam treated her kindly, and she soon forgot all about her former comrade.

Poor Doggie did not fare so well. Indeed, he had a rough time. He wandered aimlessly about over the frozen ground and could not find the slightest scrap of food. After three days, weary, paw-sore and dispirited, he came to a wolf's lair and begged for shelter. The wolf took pity on him, gave him some scraps of food, and permitted him to sleep in the lair. Doggie was most thankful, and sleeping with his ears on the alert, he heard stealthy footsteps in the night. He told the wolf.

"Drive the intruders away," said his host in a surly tone.

Doggie went out obediently to do so. But the marauders were wild animals and they nearly killed him. He was lucky to escape with his life. After bathing his wounds at a pool in the early morning he wandered all day long, but again could find nothing. Toward night, when he could scarcely drag his famished and wounded body along, he saw a monkey in a tree.

"Kind monkey," he pleaded, "give me shelter for the night. I am exhausted and starving."

"Go away, go away, go away," chattered the monkey, jumping and swinging swiftly from branch to branch, moving his lips quickly and opening and shutting his eyes comically. Doggie hesitated, and, to frighten him away, the monkey pulled cocoanuts from the tree and pelted him.

Poor Doggie crawled miserably away.

"What shall I do?" he moaned.

Hearing the bleating of some sheep, he made his way to them and asked them to take compassion on him.

"We will," they replied, "if you will keep watch over us and tell us when the wolf comes."

Doggie agreed willingly, and, after he had devoured some food, he stretched himself to sleep like a faithful watch-dog, with one eye open.

In the middle of the night he heard the wolves approaching, and, anxious to serve the sheep who had treated him kindly, he sprang to his feet and began to bark loudly. This aroused the sheep, who awoke and started to run in all directions. Some of them ran right into the pack of wolves and were killed and eaten. Poor Doggie was nearly heart-broken.

"It is my fault, my fault," he wailed. "I barked too soon. Oh, what an unhappy creature I am. I shall keep away from all animals now."

Once again he set off on his travels. Whenever he met an animal he ran off in the opposite direction. He had to make his journey by the loneliest paths and the most unfrequented routes, and the difficulty of finding food grew steadily greater. At last he grew so weak and thin that he hardly had strength to crawl and he had several narrow escapes from falling as prey to ferocious beasts.

One night he came to a house and begged a morsel of food. It was given, and during the night he woke the man and warned him that wild animals were making a raid. The man jumped up, seized his bow and arrow and drove the thieves away. Then he patted Doggie.

"Good dog," he said. "You are a wise animal. Stay with me always. You will find Father Adam kind."

"Father Adam!" cried Doggie, in alarm. "I must not stay here."

"Nonsense. I say you must," answered Adam, and Doggie was compelled to obey.

In the morning, Pussie learned that the dog had joined the household and she complained to Adam.

"The dog has violated the oath he swore not to come to the place where I am," she said.

"He did not know you were here," said Adam, wanting to keep the peace. "He is very useful. I want him to remain. He won't hurt you. There is ample room for both."

"No, there isn't," said Puss spitefully, arching up her back and getting cross. "He broke his oath. He is a wicked creature. You dare not overlook his offense."

Poor Doggie stood dejectedly apart, with his tail between his legs.

"I didn't know it was Adam's house, and I was so hungry and miserable and tired," he said.

But Pussie would not be pacified. She thrust out her ugly claws and tried to scratch her former partner. The dog kept out of her way as much as possible, but she quarrelled with him at every opportunity, and at last he determined to tolerate her conduct no longer.

"I must leave you, Father Adam," he said. "Pussie is making my life unbearable."

"But I want you," said Adam.

"I'm sorry," said Doggie, firmly, "but it is really impossible for me to continue in your service. I've got another situation at the house of Seth. He wants me, too."

"Won't you make friends with Pussie?" asked Adam.

"With pleasure, if she will let me, but she won't."

"You blame each other," said Adam, losing patience. "I can't make you out. You look like quarrelling for ever."

Adam's words have proved true. Ever since that time the cat and dog have failed to agree, and Pussie will never consent to be friendly again with Doggie.

A Wise Weaver

This story has been adapted from Abraham G. Seklemian's version of the same tale that originally appeared in The Golden Maiden and Other Folk Tales and Fairy Stories Told in Armenia, published in 1898 by The Helman-Taylor Company, New York. This tale is based on earlier work undertaken by Ohannes Chatschumian, who, before his death, had begun a compilation of 'Armenian' folklore for Miss Alice Fletcher. These 'Armenian' tales themselves originated in the Byzantine peasant tradition that developed over the preceding fifteen hundred years.

A king was once sitting upon his throne when an ambassador from a distant country approached, drew a line around the throne, and sat down without speaking a word. The King did not understand this mystery. He called his ministers. They also did not understand it. It was a disgrace to the King that he did not have a man wise enough to understand the symbolical message of a neighboring sovereign. The King was very angry, and ordered his ministers to solve the riddle themselves, or to find someone in the city to solve it immediately; otherwise he would put them all to death. Thereupon the ministers began to search through the realm for a wise man.

After a long quest they came to a certain house, which they entered. There was no one in the first room but a baby sleeping in a cradle.

And strange to say, the cradle was rocking without any visible cause. They entered the adjacent room, and there also was a baby sleeping in a cradle, which was rocking, though no one was in the room. They walked out into the back yard, where they saw wheat washed and spread to dry, and there was a cane moving to and fro, driving away the sparrows, in order that they might not eat the wheat. The King's ministers were surprised, and going down into the cellar they found a weaver weaving cloth.

As his wife had died soon after giving birth to twins, he had both to weave for his living and do a housewife's work and nurse his children. He had connected the two cradles and the sparrow driver to his loom and shuttle with cords, and so, in this manner, by virtue of his cleverness he was performing all his duties without much trouble. The ministers thought that this man might solve the King's riddle, and so they told him what had happened. The weaver thought a while and then taking a couple of marbles and a chicken, went with the ministers.

Entering the presence of the King, he looked the foreign ambassador in the face, and threw before him the marbles. The ambassador took from his pocket a handful of grain and spread it on the floor. The weaver put down the chicken, which in a few minutes ate all the grain. Thereupon the ambassador put on his sandals and ran away speedily.

"What was all this?" asked the King.

"By drawing the line around the throne," answered the weaver, "the ambassador wished to say that their King was coming to besiege us, if we did not humiliate ourselves and pay tribute. To this I answered by dropping marbles, which meant that they were children compared to ourselves and that they would better go and play marbles, rather than to undertake a war which would result in their utter ruin. By spreading the handful of grain he meant that their forces were innumerable. By the chicken which ate all the grain, I meant that a company of ours was enough to destroy a legion of theirs."

The King was pleased with the weaver, and gave him costly presents, but the weaver took only a little to enable him to bring up his beloved twins. The King wanted to make him his prime minister, but the weaver declined, saying, "Let me continue to be a weaver. All I ask is that you remember that wisdom and understanding are not distributed according to rank and that the common tradesmen are entitled to be treated as humanely as your peers and noblemen."

The World's Beauty

This story has been adapted from Abraham G. Seklemian's version of the same tale that originally appeared in The Golden Maiden and Other Folk Tales and Fairy Stories Told in Armenia, published in 1898 by The Helman-Taylor Company, New York. This tale is based on earlier work undertaken by Ohannes Chatschumian, who, before his death, had begun a compilation of 'Armenian' folklore for Miss Alice Fletcher. These 'Armenian' tales themselves originated in the Byzantine peasant tradition that developed over the preceding fifteen hundred years.

A rich merchant of the city of Baghdad had accumulated great wealth and property. He had a wife and a son. One day the merchant fell sick, and felt that he was about to die. On his deathbed he called his son, saying, "You see, my son, I have accumulated so great wealth that even princes have not as much. I bequeath all to you. Continue my business and enjoy your property, but never go to the city of Tiflis."

Then he called his wife, explained to her the mystery of his riches, and gave her the key to his secret chamber, saying, "If my son spends all my wealth and becomes poor, then you may tell him my secrets."

The merchant died, and his son, continuing his business, one day took forty camel-loads of merchandise, and set out for the city of

Erzerum. In the caravansary, where he deposited his goods in Erzerum, he met two poor men in rags, sighing and beating their breasts.

"What is the matter with you?" asked the young merchant.

"Oh!" exclaimed the two ragamuffins, "It is something that cannot be told."

The lad had great compassion for them, and said, "No, masters, tell me your grief. I am ready to spend all my wealth for your sake."

At last they said, "Would to heaven you had not met us, sir! You will be like ourselves."

"How?" asked the lad.

"Each of us was a wealthy merchant, such as you are," said the men. "We went to Tiflis and heard that the King had a daughter called the World's Beauty. We wished to see her, and they charged each of us forty pieces of gold to behold her from behind a glass partition. We fell in love with her, and thereafter spent all our wealth to see her over and over again. So we wasted eighty camel-loads of merchandise and today we are so poor that no one cares to look at us."

The lad gave them a handful of gold coins, and on the next day loaded his camels and started for Tiflis. He gave forty gold coins to see the World's Beauty from behind the glass, and after that spent all his wealth and merchandise for her sake. He came back to Baghdad to his mother, as poor as Job, and told her his ill-luck. She scolded him for his disobedience to his father's command. But the lad wept and promised that he would not go to Tiflis anymore, if she gave him from his father's secret chamber something by which he could earn his living and preserve his father's reputation. His mother gave him an empty purse, saying, "If today you put in this purse forty pieces of copper, on the morrow you will see that they have changed to forty pieces of gold. After three years, the gold put into the purse changes into copper. That is to say, once in three years the talisman changes to its contrary."

"This is good," thought the lad, "I now have an inexhaustible revenue, which never requires work."

He soon forgot his promise to his mother, and took the first caravan to go to Tiflis. He paid forty gold pieces every day to see the World's Beauty, and his money was not exhausted. The maiden was surprised, and one day invited him to a banquet, with the intention of robbing him.

"Ah! I love you very much," she said to him, artfully, "I will certainly marry you if you tell me the secret of your wealth."

How easily may a simple youth be deceived! The lad fell into the trap and showed her the magic purse. The maiden intoxicated him with poisonous wine, and taking away the purse expelled him from her house. He returned to his mother, lamenting his loss. He wept and promised not to go again to Tiflis, if she gave him something else from his father's secret chamber by which he might earn his living. A mother's heart is tender, and she could not resist his importunities, and at last brought to him from the secret chamber a cap, saying, "This is a magic cap. When you put it on your head you will see others without being seen by anybody."

This was something that suited the lad best of all. As soon as he became the owner of the cap he forgot his solemn promises to his mother and directly set out for the city of Tiflis. He entered the maiden's house and looked at her as much as he pleased, without being molested. The maiden and the inmates of the house detected that there was somebody in the house, but they could not see him, despite their repeated efforts. One day, the maiden thought it might be the youth of Baghdad who was playing this trick, and she called him by his name, saying, "Disclose yourself, I will certainly marry you."

The lad took the cap from his head, and appeared to the maiden.

"O, my dear lord," said the wily maiden, "I have been burning for your love. Ever since you have gone away I have uttered no name but yours, and I am yours still if you tell me your secret."

The lad was deceived by her artful words and told her the secret of the cap. A banquet was given to the lad, poisonous wine was served to him, and the cap being taken from him he was expelled from the house, with disgrace. He came back to Baghdad, begging his way. He had no heart to go again to his mother. He entreated the intervention of friends and kinsfolk, who persuaded the mother and reconciled her with her prodigal son. He begged his mother for a third secret from his father's chamber.

"Only one secret is left," she said. "If you lose this one, we shall become hungry and naked, and become paupers."

She gave the lad a horn, and told him to blow it. The lad blew it, and the mountains and plains were covered with soldiers.

"Now," she said, "blow it from the other end."

He did so, and the army disappeared.

"Mamma," said the lad, "now let me go fight with my enemies and bring back all that I have lost."

Thus speaking he set out without waiting for an answer. As soon as he arrived at Tiflis, he stood upon the hilltop near the city and blew the horn. In the twinkling of an eye the city was besieged by an army so great that there was no room left for the soldiers to stand on. There was a sudden panic in the city. All the people were terrified. The King sent messengers to the lad, asking him what he wanted.

"War! War!" exclaimed the lad. "Who do you think I am?"

They recognized him and saw that he was the lad of Baghdad. Thereupon the King called his daughter, saying, "You are the cause of this trouble. Go see the lad and quench this fire, before we both perish."

The maiden sent a messenger to the lad, saying, "I will come to you, my love, and we will go directly to the church to be married, and then go to our house. But, love, disperse your army that I may come to you."

Soon after the message the maiden herself appeared. The lad blew the horn from the other end, and the army disappeared. The maiden came to the lad, apologized for the past and poured out all her store of sweet and fascinating words. She also brought a letter from her father approving of their marriage. The lad told the maiden the secret of the horn, but this time did not give it to her.

"Well, then," said the maiden, "put the horn in your trunk, lock and seal it, and let us send it home. One cannot go to church with a horn in one's pocket. It is a sin. After the wedding we will return home, examine the seal of the trunk, and open it. Nobody will steal your horn."

The lad consented, and putting the horn in the box, sealed it and sent it to the maiden's house. When they reached the church door, the maiden suddenly exclaimed, "Oh me! I forgot to kiss the hand of my father and mother. Let me go and bid them farewell, then I will come and the wedding will take place."

The lad believed her and let her go. Coming to the house, she ordered her servants to break the trunk. She got out the horn, sent a man to the lad and expelled him with disgrace from the city. The lad was now at a complete loss. He had no more hope in his mother, and no favour in the sight of his countrymen. For a time he wandered here and there and then decided to go to sea.

"Let me go," he thought, "to the end of the world, to an unknown country, where nobody will know me."

He was accepted as a servant on board a ship. But soon after they sailed there was a heavy storm on the sea, and the ship was wrecked. The lad was saved on a piece of board, and was cast upon an uninhabited island where he lived eating wild berries. One day he saw two apple-trees growing near one another; the fruit of one was of common size, but the fruit of the other tree was as large as a man's head, and very tempting to eat.

"What a nice fruit!" thought the lad, and ate one of the large apples. As soon as he tasted it, he became a donkey, with a tail and very long ears. As a four-legged beast, for a time he grazed in the neighbourhood, only he was conscious that he was a man and had become a donkey. One day, as he was grazing near the two apple-trees, he ate one of the small apples which had fallen down from the tree, and he became a man as before.

"This is good," thought the lad, "I can make good use of these wonderful fruits."

He picked up a good many of the apples of both kinds. One day he saw a ship sailing at a distance. He displayed a signal and the ship sailed to the island. He went on board, taking both kinds of apples with him. The sailors pitied him and brought him back to Tiflis without charge. The lad disguised himself, and taking the shape of a peddler, went to the neighbourhood of the house of the King's daughter, to sell his large apples. The maiden was greatly pleased with the appearance of the fruit, and paying twenty pieces of gold, bought two large apples. She and her forty maids ate slices of the apples, and all of them were suddenly changed into donkeys, and went out into the yard braying. It is said that as a donkey also the World's Beauty was excellent. The King came with his peers who, seeing what had happened, were greatly surprised and grieved. By this time the lad was again disguised, taking the shape of a doctor, and calling himself Dr. Karabobo. The King's servants summoned all the doctors of the city, but it was of no avail. At last they said to the King that there was left only a certain Dr. Karabobo, a foreigner.

"Bring him here," said the King.

By that time all the followers of secret arts crowded about the King's palace. Priests, monks, astrologers, star-gazers, magicians, sorcerers, witches, wizards, necromancers, bird conjurers, mice conjurers, snake conjurers, predictors by measuring with the span, predictors by casting beans or blue pebbles, predictors by gazing at cups of water, and all kinds of enchanters, male and female, old and young, were there, practicing their arts, but none could understand the secret, or devise a remedy. They all, however, were unanimous in declaring that it was a punishment sent from heaven to chastise the World's Beauty for her arbitrary cruelties.

Then Dr. Karabobo came in and said to the King, "I can transform these donkeys once more into human beings, but only on two conditions. First you must give me your daughter in marriage, and secondly, you must give me whatever else I might desire."

"I agree to do so," answered the King.

The agreement was written, signed and sealed by the King and his twelve peers. The lad took the document, and putting it in his pocket, said, "First of all, I want you to bring here the eighty camel-loads of merchandise, which your daughter stole from two merchants."

The King gave orders and they were brought.

"Now bring," he added, "the forty loads which were taken from the youth of Baghdad. Bring his magic purse, cap, and horn, and also the gold coins which were, during the past years, taken from the magic purse at the rate of forty gold pieces a day."

The King and his lords were surprised that he knew all this, but were obliged to bring what he asked, according to the agreement. The King only begged him not to demand the gold which the purse had held, as there was not enough in the royal treasury to make up so large a sum. But Dr. Karabobo was inflexible. He held the horn in readiness to call the army, if needed. Then he drew the small apples out of his pocket and gave a piece to every donkey, whereupon they were transformed into human beings. After that he told them who he was.

He took the maiden and all belonging to him and set out for Baghdad. He blew the horn and an immense army accompanied him. Thus with a princely procession he came to the city of Erzerum, where he found the two ex-merchants and restored to them their property. Then he entered Baghdad with great pomp, and said to his mother, who had gone to meet him, "Mother, here are all my possessions, and here is the maiden who tortured your son so much. I was obliged to become an ass before I learned how to treat her, and it was necessary for her to become an ass before she ceased to be a deceitful shrew. She is now a human being and promises to become a faithful daughter-in-law."

The maiden then kissed both hands of the aged woman as a token of her obedience. They celebrated their wedding festival for forty days, after which they went to the church and were married.

The Story Of Bostanai

This story has been adapted from Gertrude Landa's version of the same tale that originally appeared in Jewish Fairy Tales and Legends, published in 1943 by Bloch Publishing Co. Inc., New York.

In the days of long ago, when Persia was a famous and beautiful land, with innumerable rose gardens that perfumed the whole country and gorgeous palaces, there lived a king, named Hormuz. He was a cruel monarch, this Shah of Persia. He tyrannized over his people and never allowed them to live in peace. Above all, he hated the Jews.

"These descendants of Abraham," he said to his grand vizier, "never know when they are beaten. I can't remember how many times it has been reported to me that they have been wiped out of existence, or driven from the land. Yet nothing, it seems, can crush their spirit. Tell me, why is this?"

"It is because they have a firm faith in their future," answered the vizier.

"What do you mean by those words?" demanded the king, angrily.

"I speak only of what I have heard from wise men," the vizier replied, hastily. "They hold the belief that they will be restored as a united people to their own land."

"Under their own king?" interrupted Hormuz.

"Under a descendant of the royal House of David," the vizier answered, solemnly.

The king stamped his foot with rage.

"How dare they think of any other Shah but me," he exclaimed, for his one idea of ruling over people was that he had every right to be cruel to them. Then he said suddenly, "Do you think that if there were no more people who could trace their ancestry to this… this David, their faith would be shattered?"

"Perhaps, it may be so."

"It shall be so," cried the king. "There shall be no remnants of this House of David."

He summoned his executioners, and when they were lined up before him, he surveyed the evil-looking band with a cunning gleam in his eye.

"To you," he said, in a rasping voice, "I hand over all the descendants of the House of David to be found among the Jews in the whole of the realm of Persia. Slay them instantly. See to it that not a single one, man, woman, or child, is left alive. Woe betide you, and you my counsellors if my commands are not carried out to the letter. To your duties. You are dismissed from my presence."

Waving them away, he indulged his fancy in thoughts of the coming executions, chuckling the while.

From day to day he received reports that his commands were being carried out. The land was filled with weeping, for the cruel butchery was worse than war. None could defend themselves. Mere suspicion was enough for the executioners. They wasted no time with doubts, but slew all who were said to belong to the House of David. The

Shah looked over the list each night and chuckled. At last he was informed that all had been slaughtered.

"'Tis well, 'tis well," he said, rubbing his hands, gleefully, "I shall sleep in peace tonight."

He slept in a bower in a rose garden, and nowhere in the world are the roses so magnificent and so sweet-scented as in Persia.

"I shall have pleasant dreams," he muttered, but instead he had a nightmare that frightened him terribly.

He dreamed that he was walking in his rose garden, but instead of deriving pleasure from the beautiful trees, he was only angered.

"Are there no white, or yellow, or pink roses?" he asked, but received no answer. "All red, deep, deep red," he muttered, in his troubled manner.

"Tell me," he demanded fiercely, stopping before a tree heavily laden with flowers, "why are you so red today?"

And the roses spoke and replied, "Because of the innocent blood that has been shed. It is royal blood that has drenched the ground, and none but crimson roses shall bloom this year in Persia."

"Bah!" screamed the enraged Shah and, drawing his scimitar, he began hacking right and left among the flowers. The beautiful blooms fell to the ground in great showers until the garden was so littered with the red petals that it seemed flooded with a pool of blood. At last only one tree remained, and as the Shah raised his sword to cut it down, an old man stepped from behind it and confronted the king.

"Who are you, and where have you come from?" the monarch asked fiercely.

The old man made no answer. Gazing sternly into the eyes of the Shah, he raised his hand suddenly and unexpectedly, and struck the king such a violent blow that he fell sprawling to the ground. He lay half-stunned among the red petals, looking up at the old man.

"Are you not satisfied with the destruction you have wrought?" the old man asked. "Must you take the life of the last rose tree?"

The old man stooped to pick up the scimitar which had fallen from the king's grasp.

"No, no," screamed Hormuz, fearing that he was to be slain. He scrambled to his knees and with clasped hands pleaded to the old man. "Do not take my life," he begged. "Spare me, and I shall spare the last tree and cherish it tenderly."

"So be it," said the old man, holding the sword above his head. It dropped to the ground, and looking up, Hormuz saw that the stranger had vanished.

The Shah awoke. His body trembled with fear, his head was wracked by a burning pain. He looked round shudderingly to see if the angry old man still stood above him with the threatening sword. Then he sent for his wizards.

"Explain my horrid dream to me," he said.

Their interpretations, however, did not please him.

"You are fools," he cried. "Go and search for a man of wisdom who understands these mysteries. Seek a sage among the Jews."

The royal servants hastened to do the king's bidding. They knew full well that when Hormuz was in a rage, lives were quickly forfeit.

They seized the aged rabbi of the city and brought him before the Shah.

"Can you interpret dreams?" asked the king, abruptly, dispensing with the usual ceremonies.

"I can explain the meaning of certain things," returned the rabbi.

"Then do not fail to unravel the mystery of my dream," said Hormuz, and he related it. "I must know the secret," he concluded, "or..." But he stopped. He was afraid to add the usual threat of death that morning.

"'Tis a simple dream," said the rabbi, slowly. "The things of which men, and even kings are only men, dream in their sleep are connected with the deeds performed by day. Your garden represents the House of David which you have sought to destroy. The old man was King David himself, and you have promised to cherish and nurture his one remaining descendant."

The Shah listened in silence. Then, with a flash in his eye he said, "But all the descendants of this King David were slain."

"All but one," said the rabbi. "There is a boy babe, born on the day the executions ceased."

"Where is he?" asked Hormuz.

"Your vow...." the rabbi began, nervously, for he did not wish to hand over this child to death.

"My promise shall be faithfully carried out," interrupted the monarch.

"The boy is in my house," said the rabbi. "His mother, who escaped the massacre, died when he was born."

"Bring him here," commanded Hormuz. "Do not be afraid."

From his finger he drew a ring and handed it to the learned man.

"This is my bond," he said. "The possession of this ensures your safety."

The child was brought to the palace, and the Shah looked at him with an intent gaze.

"He shall be brought up as a prince," said the king. "He shall have servants, attendants and slaves in great number to minister to all his needs. He shall be treated with the utmost kindness. And because of my dream in the garden, I name him Bostanai."

The Shah did this because "bostan" is the Persian word for rose garden.

He touched the child with his jewelled sceptre and all present bowed low before the babe and showed him the respect and devotion due to a prince.

Hormuz, however, was too cruel to be quite satisfied. He feared to harm the boy, but he wanted some proof that Bostanai was really a descendant of King David. The child grew up into a handsome, clever youth, and Hormuz, partly out of fear, but partly because he had really grown to love the boy, kept him constantly by his side.

One day, while sitting in the bower in the garden, he watched the boy among the roses. The day was hot and a drowsiness came over the king. He had not slept in that bower since the night of his fateful dream, and he was not happy about doing so now. But he did not lack courage, and he called the boy to him.

"Bostanai," he said, "stand guard by the door, and do not move while I sleep."

Hormuz slept soundly and peacefully for some time, and when he awoke he saw the lad standing motionless where he had placed himself.

"Bostanai," he called, and when the boy turned, he was startled to see blood trickling from a wound on his face.

"What is that?" he asked, anxiously.

"The sting of a wasp," Bostanai replied.

"Is it not painful?"

For answer, the boy only smiled.

"How did it happen?" asked the king.

"The wasp stung me while I stood guard."

"But could you not brush it away?"

"No," replied the boy, proudly. "King David was my ancestor, and in the presence of a king I must stand motionless until bidden to make any movement."

Then, before the king could catch him, he swooned from loss of blood, and fell to the ground. He soon recovered, however, and the Shah's doubts were set at rest.

"I know now you are truly of the House of David," he said, "for none other could have shown such fortitude."

Bostanai became the Shah's favourite, and when he grew up he was made the ruler of a province. He lived happily, and through him the Jews of the land also lived in prosperity and peace.

A Son Of Anak

This story has been adapted from Henry Wysham Lanier's version of the same tale that originally appeared in A Book of Giants, published in 1922 by E. P. Dutton and Company, New York.

There was war for many years between the children of Israel and the Philistines.

It came to pass while Saul was King that the Philistines gathered together a great army, and marched into the land of Judah against the Israelites, and encamped in a plain near Shochoh. Saul also drew out his army and hurried forward, and occupied a hill overlooking this plain, whereupon the Philistines were forced to leave their position and to establish themselves on another hill across the valley of Elah from Saul's camp.

While the armies faced each other, one day a champion named Goliath came out from the ranks of the Philistines. He was very terrible to behold, for he was of the race of those sons of Anak for fear of whom the Israelites under Moses had murmured and had been therefore condemned to wander forty years in the wilderness. And while Joshua had finally led them across the Jordan after the death of Moses, and had fought the Anakim and overcome them, there had remained three cities where their descendants still dwelt; Gaza, and

Gath and Ashdod. It was from Gath that this Goliath had come with the invading army.

He was half as tall again as an ordinary man, something over nine feet. His bronze breastplate alone weighed as much as a man, and on his head was a helmet of brass, and he carried over his shoulder a mighty spear which looked like a weaver's beam, and the head of which alone weighed twenty-five pounds. Bronze greaves were upon his legs, and he bore a shield of gleaming brass.

This daunting figure advanced boldly into the plain, between the two armies drawn up in battle array, and in a great voice cried out, "Why have you come here to set your army for battle? I am a Philistine and you are servants of Saul? Choose your champion and let him come down to fight me.

"If he is able to fight with me, and to kill me, then will we be your servant, but if I prevail against him and kill him, then shall you be our servants. I defy the armies of Israel. Give me a man, that we may fight together."

Now this was quite customary in the olden times. Many a great issue had been decided by the combat of two champions. Moreover, there were brave men enough in the army of the Israelites, for Saul had fought wars all of his life, against the children of Moab and the Amalekites, against Ammon, Edom and Zoab, and when he had seen any strong or valiant fighter among his people, he had straightway taken him under his wing. But at the sight of this huge, brazen warrior, his hardiest veterans turned pale and trembled, for it was a saying passed on from father to son for many generations, "Who shall stand before the sons of Anak?"

So, among all those thousands no one so much as answered the giant's challenge, to which, when he perceived this, he reviled them and returned to his own people.

The next day he came forth again, morning and evening, and the day after that, and each day following, always repeating his challenge in the face of all the force, and taunting them bitterly. Saul was greatly troubled, for he knew well that this open fear of the giant would affect his soldiers, when battle was joined. He offered, therefore, great riches to any man who would go forth against the challenger, and whoever should slay him should have the king's daughter in marriage, and his father's house should be free in Israel. Yet even this could not prevail upon any to stand before the Philistine, so that for forty days Goliath braved and insulted the whole army without response.

Now there were three brothers among those who followed Saul, Eliab, Abinadab and Shammah. They were sons of Jesse, who dwelt ten or twelve miles from the battlefield in the hills near Bethlehem. This Jesse had a fourth son, David, who was but a stripling and tended his father's sheep.

He was a ruddy youth, of fair gaze, and beautiful to look upon. He was a cunning musician and when an evil spirit of melancholy descended upon the king, one of his servants brought the boy to play the harp for his master. The youth's skill in charming away this evil spirit gave him favour in Saul's sight, so that he kept him by his side and made him his armour-bearer for a time. But when the three older sons of Jesse joined the army gathered against the Philistines, David then returned to his duties with his father's flocks.

It chanced at this time that Jesse called David to him, saying, "Take this bushel of parched corn and these ten loaves and carry them swiftly to the camp to your brothers. And carry these ten cheeses to the captain of their thousand, and see how your brothers fare and bring me word again."

So David arose very early in the morning and left the sheep with a keeper and went as his father had commanded to the camp by the valley of Elah. It was an easy journey for one who spent his days abroad with the sheep, and the sun was only just up when he reached the encampment.

All was noise and confusion as he arrived, for both hosts were setting themselves in battle array, army against army. So the youth left his burdens with the keeper of the supplies, and ran in among the ranks until he found his brothers and said to them, "Peace be with you."

As he talked with them, the Philistine champion appeared on the opposite slope. According to his usual practice, he challenged the whole army and reviled them, while the men of Israel drew back, afraid as before.

David heard these insults, and also heard the talk of those who stood by. He heard about the great things King Saul had promised to any who might overthrow the giant, and how long his boast and defiance had gone unquestioned.

"What will happen," he inquired of his neighbours, "to the man that killed this Philistine and takes away the reproach from Israel? Who is this Philistine that he should defy the armies of the living God?"

They answered and told him what the king had promised.

His eldest brother Eliab heard these questions, and he grew angry with David. He turned upon him, saying, "Why have you come down here? And with whom have you left our sheep in the wilderness? I know your pride and forwardness. You have come down so that you might see the battle."

"What have I done now?" replied the youth. "There was good reason for my coming?"

He turned away and again asked the nearest soldier about thew whole affair, receiving the same answer. And some one came to Saul, relating the words the stripling had spoken. Saul sent for him.

As soon as he stood in the king's presence, David broke out, pointing to the distant figure of the giant, "Let no man's heart fail because of him. I, your servant, will go and fight with this Philistine."

"You are not able to go against this Philistine to fight with him," answered Saul, "for you are but a youth, and he is a man of war from his childhood up."

"Your servant kept his father's sheep," urged the young man, "and a lion came and a bear and took a lamb out of the flock. And I went out after the lion and hit him and delivered the lamb out of his mouth: and when he rose up against me, I caught him by the hair and hit him again, and slew him. I, your servant, slew both the lion and the bear. This Philistine shall be like the lion and the bear. He has defied the armies of the living God."

When Saul saw the eagerness and confidence of this handsome young shepherd, he was reminded of the deed of his son Jonathan when, accompanied only by his armour-bearer, he had climbed up into the enemy's garrison at Michmash, and slain twenty men within the space of half an acre, and started the rout of the whole army of the Philistines which had been about to overrun the land.

"Go," said he, "and the Lord be with you."

So he armed David with his own armour and put a helmet on his head. And David buckled on the king's sword and tried to walk; but he was so unaccustomed to the armour that he said to the king, "I cannot go with these. I cannot use them."

So he removed the armour, and set out in his shepherd's clothes, with his staff in his hand and his sling hanging from his belt. The sling was the weapon he knew best, and it was by no means to be despised. The plain piece of leather with thongs attached to each end, by means of which a stone could be hurled, was perhaps the very earliest means of fighting at a distance, and it was the traditional weapon of more than one nation of the Syrian region. When the Benjaminites fought with Israel, there were 700 chosen sling-men, left-handed, every one of whom could sling stones at a hair's-breadth and not miss. An expert slinger had the advantage, against a warrior armed with sword and spear, of being able to deliver an attack long before he himself was threatened.

The youth walked to the brook and carefully selected five round stones of the right size, which he put into the wallet slung over his shoulder. Then, in full sight of both armies, he advanced against the giant warrior, who stood brandishing his great spear and shouting his scorn.

Seeing David approach, he came forward, preceded by his shield-bearer. But seeing only this fresh-faced stripling in his skin garment, he was filled with contempt at such an antagonist.

"Am I a dog," he cried, "that you comes to me with staves?"

Cursing the youth by his heathen gods, he shouted, "Come to me, and I will give your flesh to the fowls of the air, and to the beasts of the field."

Calmly David answered, "You come to me with a sword and with a spear, and with a shield, but I come to you in the name of the Lord of hosts, the God of the armies of Israel, whom you have defied.

"This day the Lord will deliver you into my hand, and I will fight you, and take your head, and I will give the carcasses of the Philistine host to the fowls of the air, and to the wild beasts of the earth. All who are assembled here will know that there is a god in Israel."

Enraged at this insolence, the Philistine champion hastened forward to kill down this boaster with one blow. But David ran towards him. And as he ran he took one of the stones and placed it in his sling. Whirling it about, he hurled it so shrewdly that the stone struck Goliath full in the forehead, burying itself in the skull.

Down crashed that giant bulk to earth. The shield-bearer fled aghast back to his own lines. Running up to his prostrate adversary, the youth drew the giant's sword from his sheath, and, while the multitude looked on in awed silence, he cut the Philistine's head from his body.

At that the Israelites set up a shout which echoed from hill to hill. The Philistine host turned and fled in utter panic, while Saul's men slaughtered them all the way to the gates of Gath, making great spoil of their belongings.

But David took the giant's sword and placed it in the sanctuary of Nob, where it was to serve him in dire need, at a later day.

And Saul set him over all his men of war.

The Palace In The Clouds

This story has been adapted from Gertrude Landa's version of the same tale that originally appeared in Jewish Fairy Tales and Legends, published in 1943 by Bloch Publishing Co. Inc., New York.

Ikkor, the Jewish vizier of the king of Assyria, was the wisest man in the land, but he was not happy. He was the greatest favourite of the king who heaped honours upon him, and the idol of the people who bowed before him in the streets and cast themselves on the ground at his feet to kiss the hem of his garment. He always had a kindly word and a smile for those who sought his advice and guidance, but his eyes were always sad, and tears would trickle down his cheeks as he watched the little children at play in the streets.

His fame as a man of wisdom was known far beyond the borders of Assyria, and rulers feared to give offense to the king who had Ikkor as the chief of his counsellors to assist in the affairs of state. But Ikkor would often sit alone in his beautiful palace and sigh heavily. No sound of children's laughter was ever heard in Ikkor's palace, and that was the cause of his sorrow. Ikkor was a pious man and deeply learned in the Holy Law, and he had prayed long and devoutly and had listened to the advice of magicians that he might be blessed with just one son, or a daughter, to carry down his name and renown. But the years passed and no child was born to him.

Every year, on the advice of the king, he married another wife, and now he had in his harem thirty wives, all childless. He determined to take no more wives, and one night he dreamed a dream in which a spirit appeared to him and said, "Ikkor, you will die full of years and honour, but childless. Therefore, take Nadan, the son of your widowed sister and let him be a son to you."

Nadan was a handsome youth of fifteen, and Ikkor related his dream to the boy's mother who permitted him to take Nadan to his palace and there bring him up as his own son. The sadness faded from the vizier's eyes as he watched the lad at his games and his lessons, and Ikkor himself imparted wisdom to Nadan. But, first to his surprise, and then to his grief, Nadan was not thankful for the riches and love lavished upon him. He neglected his lessons and grew proud, haughty and arrogant. He treated the servants of the household harshly and did not obey the wise maxims of Ikkor.

The vizier, however, was hopeful that he would reform and gain wisdom with years, and he took him to the palace of the king and appointed him an officer of the royal guard. For Ikkor's sake, the king made Nadan one of his favourites, and everyone in the land looked upon the young man as the successor to Ikkor and the future vizier. This only served to make Nadan still more arrogant, and a wicked idea entered his head to gain further favour with the king and supplant Ikkor at once.

"Oh King, live for ever!" he said one day, when Ikkor was absent in a distant part of the land. "It grieves me to have to utter words of warning against Ikkor, the wise, the father who has adopted me. But he conspires to destroy you."

The king laughed at this suggestion, but he became serious when Nadan promised to give him proof in three days. Nadan then set to work and wrote two letters. One was addressed to Pharaoh, king of Egypt, and read as follows:

"Pharaoh, son of the Sun and mighty ruler on earth, live for ever! You would reign over Assyria. Give ear then to my words and on the tenth day of the next month come with your troops to the Eagle Plain beyond the city, and I, Ikkor, the grand vizier, will deliver your enemy, the King of Assyria, into your hands."

To this letter he forged Ikkor's name, and then he took it to the king.

"I have found this," he said, "and have brought it to you. It shows you that Ikkor would deliver this country to your enemy."

The king was very angry and would have sent for Ikkor at once, but Nadan counselled patience.

"Wait until the tenth of next month, the day of the annual review, and you will see what will surprise you still more," he said.

Then he wrote the second letter. This was to Ikkor and was forged with the king's name and sealed with the king's seal which he obtained. It bade Ikkor on the tenth of the next month to assemble the troops on the Eagle Plain to show how numerous they were to the foreign envoys and to pretend to attack the king, so as to demonstrate how well they were drilled.

The vizier returned the day before the review, and while the king stood with Nadan and the foreign envoys, Ikkor and the troops, acting on their instructions, made a pretence of attacking his majesty.

"Do you not see?" said Nadan. "The king of Egypt not being here, Ikkor threatens you," and he immediately gave orders to the royal trumpeters to sound "Halt!"

Ikkor was brought before the king and confronted with the letter to Pharaoh.

"Explain this, if you can," exclaimed the king, angrily. "I have trusted you and loaded you with riches and honours and you would betray me. Is not this your signature, and is not your seal appended?"

Ikkor was too much astounded to reply, and Nadan whispered to the king that this proved his guilt.

"Lead him to the execution," cried the king, "and let his head be severed from his body and cast one hundred ells away."

Falling on his knees, Ikkor pleaded that at least he should be granted the privilege of being executed within his own house so that he might be buried there.

This request was granted, and Nabu Samak, the executioner, led Ikkor as a prisoner to his palace. Nabu Samak was a great friend to Ikkor and it grieved him to have to carry out the king's order.

"Ikkor," he said, "I am certain that you are innocent, and I would save you. Listen to me. In the prison is a wretched highwayman who has committed murder and who deserves death. His beard and hair are like yours, and at a little distance he can easily be mistaken for you. I will behead him and I will show his head to the crowd, while you can hide and live in secret."

Ikkor thanked his friend and the plan was carried out. The robber's head was exhibited to the crowd from the roof of the house and the people wept because they thought it was the head of the good Ikkor. Meanwhile, the vizier descended into a cellar deep beneath his palace and lived there, while his adopted son, Nadan, was appointed chief of the king's counsellors in his stead.

Now, when Pharaoh, king of Egypt, heard that Ikkor, the wise, had been executed, he determined to make war upon Assyria. Therefore, he dispatched a letter to the king, asking him to send an architect to design and build a palace in the clouds.

"If you do this," he wrote, "I, Pharaoh, son of the Sun, will pay you tribute. If you fail, you must pay me tribute."

The king of Assyria was perplexed when he received this letter which had to be answered in three months. Nadan could not advise him what to do, and he bitterly regretted that Ikkor, the man of wisdom, was no longer by his side to advise him.

"I would give one-fourth of my kingdom to bring Ikkor to life again," he exclaimed.

Hearing these words, Nabu Samak, the executioner, fell on his knees and confessed that Ikkor was alive.

"Bring him here at once," cried the king.

Ikkor could scarcely credit the truth when his friend came to him in the cellar with the news, and the people wept tears of joy and pity when the old vizier was led through the streets. He presented a most extraordinary spectacle.

For twelve months he had been immured in the cellar and his beard had grown down to the ground, his hair descended below his shoulders and his fingernails were several inches long. The king wept, too, when he saw his old vizier.

"Ikkor," he said, "for months I have I felt that you were innocent, and I have missed your wise counsels. Help me in my difficulty and you shall be pardoned."

"Your majesty," said Ikkor, "I desire nothing more than to serve you. I am innocent. Time will prove me guiltless."

When he saw Pharaoh's demand, he smiled.

"'Tis easy," he said. "I will go to Egypt and outwit Pharaoh."

He gave orders that four of the tame eagles in the gardens of the palace should be brought to him with cords five hundred ells long attached to their claws. Then he selected four lithe youths and trained them to sit on the backs of the eagles and soar aloft. This done, he set out for Egypt with a big caravan and a long retinue of slaves.

"What is your name?" asked Pharaoh when he presented himself.

"My name is Akbam, and I am but the lowest of my king's advisers."

"Does your master then think my demand so simple?" asked Pharaoh.

Ikkor bowed to indicate that this was so, and Pharaoh was much annoyed and puzzled.

"Perform your task at once," he commanded.

At a sign from Ikkor, the four youths mounted the eagles which flew aloft to the extremity of their cords. The birds remained in the air two hundred ells apart, as they had been trained, and the lads held cords in the form of a square.

"That is the plan of the palace in the clouds," said Ikkor, pointing aloft. "Bid your men carry up bricks and mortar. The task is so simple that the boys will build."

Pharaoh frowned. He had not expected to be thus outwitted, but he would not immediately acknowledge this.

"In this land," he said, sarcastically, "we use no mortar. We sew the stones together. Can you do this?"

"Easily," replied Ikkor, "if your wise men can make me a thread of sand."

"And can you weave a thread of sand?" asked Pharaoh.

"I can," responded Ikkor.

Noting the direction of the sun, he bored a tiny hole in the wall, and a thin sunbeam gleamed through. Then, taking a few grains of sand he blew them through the hole and in the sunbeam they seemed like a thread. "Take it, quickly," he cried, but of course nobody could do this.

Pharaoh looked long and earnestly at Ikkor.

"Truly, you are a man of wisdom," he said. "If he were not dead I should say you were Ikkor, the wise."

"I am Ikkor," answered the vizier, and he told the story of his escape.

"I will prove your innocence," exclaimed Pharaoh. "I will write a letter to your royal master."

Not only did he do so, but he gave Ikkor many valuable presents and the vizier returned to Assyria, resumed his place by the king's side, and became a greater favourite than before. Nadan was banished and was never heard of again.

The Sparrow And The Two Children

This story has been adapted from Abraham G. Seklemian's version of the same tale that originally appeared in The Golden Maiden and Other Folk Tales and Fairy Stories Told in Armenia, published in 1898 by The Helman-Taylor Company, New York. This tale is based on earlier work undertaken by Ohannes Chatschumian, who, before his death, had begun a compilation of 'Armenian' folklore for Miss Alice Fletcher. These 'Armenian' tales themselves originated in the Byzantine peasant tradition that developed over the preceding fifteen hundred years.

Vart was the name of a boy who was six years old, and Vartoohi was the name of his sister, who was five years of age. Varteni, their dear mother, had died, and Vartan, their father, had brought home a stepmother who had a boy of her own who was four years old. Vartan was a well-to-do farmer, and as he loved his children he brought them nice suits of clothes and dresses, delicious food, pretty toys and many other presents. The stepmother, being a wicked woman, envied the little half-orphans and wished to destroy them so that she might secure every good thing for her own child. In order to attain her vile purpose she secretly boiled the seed which her husband was to sow in the field that year. The wheat, of course, did not grow, and as there was no crop, the farmer had to borrow to meet his expenses. The following year she played the same treacherous trick and increased the farmer's indebtedness so much that the poor man, giving up every hope of the farm, went away to work in other countries to earn money. That was what the wicked woman desired with all her heart. She fed her son with meat and pies, while she gave the half-orphans only a handful of boiled wheat to eat. One day she decided to take Vart and Vartoohi to the river as if to bathe them, and there to drown them. That day the two innocent half-orphans had taken their handful of boiled wheat and were eating it in a corner of the yard. They saw a small sparrow which was jumping and hopping around them, and chirping and chattering as it leaped. Vart wanted to kill it with a stone, but Vartoohi prevented him. As they were eating their poor, scanty meal, they listened to the little birdie, and they thought they could understand what it was chirping.

"Orphans, orphans! Good little orphans!" the little sparrow was saying, "give me a few grains which I may take to my little ones in my tiny nest and I will give you good advice."

The children cast a few grains to the bird, which after taking them to its nest came back, saying, "Orphans, run! Orphans, run! Your stepmother will take you to the river to drown you today. Run, orphans, run!"

And the little sparrow flew away. Soon the stepmother came, saying, "Get up, you dirty things! We will go to the river, where I will bathe you."

"You go first, mamma. We will come by and by," answered the orphans.

And following the advice of their little feathered friend they ran away to the mountains. The stepmother never searched for them, and the two children wandered in the forest until evening. At nightfall they entered the hollow trunk of an old sycamore tree, repeated the prayer which they had learned from their dead mother, and lay down to sleep embracing one another. Soon after daybreak the faithful sparrow came, and the two children waking heard it chirp to them, "Orphans, good orphans, come and eat. There is boiled wheat for you."

They immediately got up and ran after the sparrow, which led them until they came to a place where an old woman brought a kettleful of boiled wheat, and emptying it under a tree, went away. A great many little sparrows were gathered. The two half-orphans sat with them at the table. The good old woman used to bring the kettleful of wheat and empty it under that tree day after day. She did this in memory of her children and grandchildren, who had died when they were young boys and girls, and whom she had loved very much. She believed that these little birdies were the spirits of her dead little ones. So these two half-orphans lived with the little sparrows for a long time.

One day as the Prince was hunting in the forest he met Vart and Vartoohi, took them with him to the palace, loved them and adopted them as his son and daughter. The children were so pretty and amiable that all the court loved them dearly. But Vart and Vartoohi were not happy.

"What is the matter with you, my children?" asked the Prince, "what is the cause of your grief?"

"We long to see our dear papa who has gone away," answered Vart.

"And we long to see the little sparrow, our benefactor," added Vartoohi.

The Prince sent out men in search of Vartan, the father of the children, and finding him, brought him home. He punished his wife for her wickedness, and embraced his children. The Prince kept him also, as a messenger in the court. But who could find the sparrow? It came by itself one day, and alighting on the window where the orphans were, chirped, "You blessed little orphans, you pitied my little ones and gave me grain, and Heaven has bestowed upon you so many bounties. May you continue to be blessed and to be happy."

The Prince liked the little sparrow for its good services and permitted it to build its nest under the eaves of the palace. All sparrows which at the present time build their nests under the eaves of houses are the descendants of that good sparrow. Let us be good even to the sparrows and they may bring good to us.

The Slave's Fortune

This story has been adapted from Gertrude Landa's version of the same tale that originally appeared in Jewish Fairy Tales and Legends, published in 1943 by Bloch Publishing Co. Inc., New York.

Ahmed was the only child of the wealthiest merchant in Damascus. His father devoted his days to doing everything possible to anticipate his wishes. The boy returned his father's love with interest, and the two lived together in the utmost happiness. They were seldom apart, the father curtailing his business journeys so that he could hastily return to Damascus, and finally restricting his affairs to those which he could perform in his own home.

For safety's sake, Ahmed, whenever he was out of his father's sight, was attended, by a big slave, Pedro, an imposing looking person, richly attired as befitted his station and duties. Pedro was a faithful servant, and he and Ahmed were the firmest friends.

When Ahmed grew up to be a youth, his father decided to send him to Jerusalem to be educated. He did so reluctantly, knowing, however, that it was the wisest course to adopt. Gently he broke the news to Ahmed, for he knew the latter would dislike leaving home. Ahmed was truly sorry to have to be parted from his father, but he kept back his tears and said bravely, "It is your wish, father, therefore I cannot question it. I know that you desire only my welfare."

"Well spoken, my son," said his father.

"May I take Pedro with me?" asked Ahmed.

"No, that would not be seemly," answered his father, gently. "It would make you appear anxious to display your wealth. Such ostentation will induce people to regard you and your father as foolish persons, possessed of more wealth than is good for the exercise of wisdom. Also, my son, your future teaching must be not confined to the learning that wise men can impart to you. You are going to the great city to learn the ways of the world, to train yourself in self-reliance, and to prepare yourself for all the duties of manhood."

The youth was somewhat disappointed to hear this. It was the first occasion, as far as his memory served him, that his father had failed to grant his wish, but he was nevertheless flattered by the prospect of quickly becoming a man, and he answered, "I bow to your wisdom, my father."

He left for Jerusalem, after bidding the merchant an affectionate farewell, and in the Holy City he applied himself diligently to his studies. He delighted his teachers with his cheerful attention to his lessons, and discovered a new source of happiness in learning things for himself from observation. Also, it was a pleasant sensation to conduct his own affairs, and in the great city, with its busy narrow thoroughfares and its wonderful buildings, he daily grew less homesick. Regularly he received letters by messengers from his father, and dutifully he returned, by the same means, long epistles, setting out all the big and little things that made up his life.

A year passed, and one day the usual message that Ahmed expected came to him in a strange hand-writing. He opened it hastily, with a foreboding of evil and alarm. The writer of the letter was one of the merchant's closest friends. He said:

"O worthy son of a most worthy father, greeting to you, and may God give you strength to hear the terrible and sad tidings which it is my sorrowful duty to convey to you. Know then that it has pleased God in his wisdom to call from this earth your saintly father, to sit with the righteous ones in Heaven. Here in the city of Damascus there is great weeping, for your honoured father was the most upright of men, a friend to all in distress, a man whose bounteous charity to the poor and unfortunate was unsurpassed. But our grief, deep and heartfelt as it is, cannot be compared to yours. We have all lost a wise counsellor, a trusty friend, a guide in all things. But you have lost more. You have lost a father. You are his only son, and on you his duties will now devolve. Know then your profound grief we share with you. We tender to you our sincere sympathy, and eagerly await your coming. You have a noble position to occupy and a tradition to continue. We, your father's friends and yours, O Ahmed, will assist you."

The young man was dumbfounded when he understood the meaning of the letter. For some moments he could not speak, but sat on the ground, weeping silently. Then, remembering his father's admonitions, he promptly took up the task of settling his affairs in Jerusalem prior to his departure for Damascus.

"I will take with me," he said, "the good rabbi who has been my religious instructor, for I am not fully prepared to undertake all the duties that will fall to my lot and need some strengthening counsel."

On arrival at Damascus he was greeted by a large concourse of people who expressed their sympathy with him and spoke in terms of highest praise of his father's benevolence.

After the funeral, Ahmed called the leading townspeople together to hear his father's will read, for he was certain that many gifts to charities would be announced. Such was the case, and there were subdued murmurs of applause when the amounts were read forth.

Then suddenly the friend who had written to the young man and was reading the will, paused. "I fear there must be a mistake," he said, in a whisper to Ahmed.

"Go on," urged the assembled people, and the man read in a strange voice, "And now, having as I hope, faithfully performed my duty to the poor, I bequeath the rest of my possessions to my devoted slave, Pedro."

"Pedro!" cried the astonished crowd.

They looked at the massive figure of the attendant, but he stood motionless and impassive, betraying no sign whatsoever of joy or surprise.

Ahmed could not conceal his bewilderment.

"Is nothing left to me?" he managed to ask.

"Yes," returned his friend, and amid a sudden silence, he continued to read, "This bequest is subject to the following proviso: that one thing be given to my son before the division of my property, the same to be selected by him within twenty-four hours of the reading of this will."

The crowd melted away with mutterings of sympathy mingled with astonishment, but out of earshot of Ahmed, all said the merchant must have been mad to draw up so absurd a testament. Ahmed himself could hardly realize the great blow that had befallen him. He consulted with his father's friend and the rabbi, but, although they re-read the document many times, they could find no fault or flaw in it.

"Legally, this is correct and in perfect order and cannot be altered," said the friend.

"My father must have made a foolish mistake and must have misplaced the two words 'son' and 'slave,'" said Ahmed, bitterly.

"That does not so appear," said the rabbi, "your father was a scholar and wise man. Don't jump to conclusions, and above all do not act rashly or without thought. I would counsel you to sleep over this matter, and in the morning we shall solve this puzzle."

Ahmed, who was exhausted with grief and rage and surprise, soon fell into a deep sleep, and when he awoke the rabbi was reciting his morning prayers.

"It is a beautiful day," he said, when he had finished. "The sun shines on your happiness, Ahmed."

Ahmed was too depressed to make any comment, nor was he completely satisfied when the rabbi assured him all would be well.

"I have pondered deeply and long over your father's words," he said. "I sat up through the night until the dawn, and I have been impelled to the conclusion that your father was truly a wise man."

Ahmed interrupted with a gesture of disapproval. The rabbi took no notice but proceeded quietly, "Your father must have feared that in your absence after his death and pending your possible delay in returning here, slaves and others might rob you of your inheritance. Pedro, I have discovered, knew of the terms of the will. By informing him and making his strange will, your father, O fortunate Ahmed, made sure of your inheritance for you."

"I don't understand," muttered Ahmed.

"It is perfectly clear," said the rabbi. "As soon as you are ready, you shall make your choice of one thing. Do as I bid you, and you shall see your father's wisdom."

Ahmed had no option but to agree. He could find no solution himself, and wretched though he felt, reason told him that his father loved him and that the rabbi was renowned for shrewdness.

The townspeople gathered early to hear Ahmed make his choice of one thing, and one only, from his father's possessions. Ahmed looked less troubled than they expected, the rabbi wore his most benign expression, and Pedro stationed himself in his usual place at the door, statuesque, obedient, and expressionless as ever. Ahmed held up his hand to obtain silence.

"Acting under the terms of my father's will," he said, solemnly, "at this moment when all, before division, belongs to his estate, I choose but one of my father's possessions. I choose Pedro, the slave."

Then everybody saw the wisdom of the strange will, for with Pedro, Ahmed became possessed of his father's vast wealth.

To Pedro, who still stood motionless, Ahmed said, "And you, my good friend, shall have your freedom and possessions sufficient to keep you in comfort for the rest of your days."

"I desire nothing but to serve you," Pedro answered, "I wish to remain the faithful attendant of one who will follow nobly in the footsteps of your father."

So everybody was satisfied.

The Old Woman And The Cat

This story has been adapted from Abraham G. Seklemian's version of the same tale that originally appeared in The Golden Maiden and Other Folk Tales and Fairy Stories Told in Armenia, published in 1898 by The Helman-Taylor Company, New York. This tale is based on earlier work undertaken by Ohannes Chatschumian, who, before his death, had begun a compilation of 'Armenian' folklore for Miss Alice Fletcher. These 'Armenian' tales themselves originated in the Byzantine peasant tradition that developed over the preceding fifteen hundred years.

Once upon a time there was an old woman who had a goat. She milked the goat every day and kept the milk in the cupboard, but a sly cat came and licked it up. One day, however, the old woman succeeded in getting hold of the cat, and cutting off her tail as a punishment, let her go.

"Meow, meow!" cried the cat, "Give me my tail!"

"Bring me my milk and I will give you your tail," said the old woman.

The cat went to the goat and said, "Goat, kind goat, do give me some milk! I will give it to the old woman and get back my tail."

"Bring me some boughs from yonder tree, and I will give you milk," answered the goat.

The cat went to the tree and said, "O good tree, do give me some boughs! I will take them to the goat, get a little milk and give it to the old woman, and get back my tail."

"Bring me some water and I will give you some boughs," answered the tree.

The cat went to the water-carrier and said, "Kind water-carrier, give me some water! I will take it to the tree and get some boughs, give them to the goat and get some milk, and give it to the old woman and get my tail."

"Bring me a pair of shoes and I will give you some water," said the water-carrier.

The cat went to the shoemaker and said, "Shoemaker, good shoemaker, do give me a pair of shoes! I will give them to the water-carrier, who will give me some water; I will take it to the tree and get some boughs for the goat. She will give me some milk, which I will take to the old woman and get my tail."

"Bring me an egg and I will give you a pair of shoes," said the shoemaker.

The cat went to the hen and said, "Hen, good hen, do lay me an egg! I will take it to the shoemaker and get a pair of shoes for the water-carrier. He will give me some water, which I will take to the tree and get some boughs for the goat. She will give me some milk, which I will take to the old woman and get my tail."

"Bring me some barley and I will lay an egg for you," answered the hen.

The cat went to the threshing-floor and said, "Threshing-floor, kind threshing-floor, do give me some barley!"

The threshing-floor said, "There, you may gather the scattered barley which my good master has left as food for the birdies and ants."

The cat gathered the barley and took it to the hen, which laid her an egg. She took the egg to the shoemaker and got a pair of shoes. She took the pair of shoes to the water-carrier and got a pailful of water for the tree. The tree gave her some boughs which she took to the goat. The goat gave her some milk which she took to the old woman.

"Here is your tail," said the old woman, "and from now on be careful not to steal my milk."

The cat took her tail and tried to stick it in its place but she could not. She tried over and over again to stick it with resin, with tar and with glue, but it was of no use. So that cat has remained tailless to this day, as a sign of her being a thief.

The moral of this story is this: Wickedness is always punished. Nothing valuable can be gotten without labour. The mark of a great sin cannot be erased.

The Fairy Frog

This story has been adapted from Gertrude Landa's version of the same tale that originally appeared in Jewish Fairy Tales and Legends, published in 1943 by Bloch Publishing Co. Inc., New York.

Once upon a time there lived a man of learning and wealth who had an only son, named Hanina. To this son, who was grown up and married, he sent a messenger asking that he should immediately come to his father. Hanina obeyed, and found both his father and mother lying ill.

"Know, my son," said the old man, "we are about to die. Grieve not, for it has been so ordained. We have been companions through life, and we are to be privileged to leave this world together. You will mourn for us the customary seven days. They will end on the eve of the festival of the Passover. On that day go to the marketplace and purchase the first thing offered to you, no matter what it is, or what the cost that may be demanded. It will in due course bring you good fortune. Listen to my words, my son, and all will be well."

Hanina promised obedience to this strange injunction of his father, and events fell out in accordance with the old man's prediction. The aged couple died on the same day, were buried together and after the week of mourning, on the day preceding the Passover festival,

Hanina made his way to the marketplace wondering what adventure was in store for him.

He had scarcely entered the marketplace, where all manner of wares were displayed, when an old man approached him, carrying a silver casket of curious design.

"Purchase this, my son," he said, "and it will bring you good fortune."

"What does it contain?" asked Hanina.

"That I may not inform you," was the reply. "Indeed I cannot, for I don't know. Only the purchaser can open it at the feast which begins the Passover."

Naturally, Hanina was impressed by these words. Matters were shaping just as his father foretold.

"What is the price?" he asked.

"A thousand gold pieces."

That was an enormous sum, nearly the whole that he possessed, but Hanina, remembering his vow, paid the money and took the casket home. It was placed upon the table that night when the Passover festival began. On being opened it was found to contain a smaller casket. This was opened and out sprang a frog.

Hanina's wife was sorely disappointed, but she gave food to the frog which devoured everything greedily. So much did the creature eat that when the Passover had ended, in eight days it had grown to an enormous size. Hanina built a cabinet for his strange possession, but it continued to grow and soon required a special shed.

Hanina was seriously puzzled, for the frog ate so ravenously that he and his wife had little food for themselves. But they made no complaint, although their hardships increased daily. They were compelled to dispose of almost everything they possessed to keep the frog supplied with food, and at last they were left in a state of abject poverty. Then the courage of Hanina's wife give way and she began to cry.

To her astonishment, the frog, which was now bigger than a man, spoke to her. "Listen to me, wife of the faithful Hanina," it said. "You have treated me well. Therefore, ask of me what you will, and I shall carry out your wishes."

"Give us food," sobbed the woman.

"It is there," said the frog, and at that very moment there was a knock at the door and a huge basket of food was delivered.

Hanina had not yet spoken, and the frog asked him to name his desire.

"A frog that speaks and performs wonders must be wise and learned," said Hanina. "I wish that you should teach me the lore of men."

The frog agreed, and his method of teaching was exceedingly strange. He wrote out the Law and the seventy known languages on strips of paper. These he ordered Hanina to swallow. Hanina did so and became acquainted with everything, even the language of the beasts and the birds. All men regarded him as the most learned sage of his time.

One day the frog spoke again.

"The day has arrived," he said, "when I must repay you for all the kindness you have shown me. Your reward shall be great. Come with me to the woods and you shall see marvels performed."

Hanina and his wife followed the giant frog to the woods very early one morning, and a comical figure it presented as it hobbled along. When they arrived at the woods, the frog cried out, in its croaking voice, "Come to me all you inhabitants of the trees, the caves and streams, and do my bidding. Bring precious stones from the depths of the earth and roots and herbs."

Then he queerest procession began. Hundreds upon hundreds of birds came twittering through the trees. Thousands upon thousands of insects came crawling from holes in the ground, and all the animals in the woods, from the tiniest to the monsters, came in answer to the call of the frog. Each group brought some gift and laid it at the feet of Hanina and his wife who stood in some alarm. Soon a great pile of precious stones and herbs was heaped before them.

"All these belong to you," said the frog, pointing to the jewels. "Of equal worth are the herbs and the roots with which you can cure all diseases. Because you obeyed the wishes of the dying and did not question me, you are now rewarded."

Hanina and his wife thanked the frog and then the former said, "May we not know who you are?"

"Yes," replied the frog. "I am the fairy son of Adam, gifted with the power of assuming any form. Farewell."

Then, the frog began to grow smaller and smaller until it was the size of an ordinary frog. Then it hopped into a stream and disappeared and all the denizens of the woods returned to their haunts.

Hanina and his wife made their way home with their treasures. They became famous for their wealth, their wisdom and their charity, and lived in happiness with all peoples for many, many years.

King Solomon And Ashmodai

This story has been adapted from Henry Iliowizi's version of the same tale that originally appeared in The Weird Orient, published in 1900 by Henry T. Coates and Company, Philadelphia.

It is well known that after Solomon had succeeded his father David as ruler over Israel he had a vision wherein the Lord gave him the choice between riches and wisdom, and that the youthful monarch gave wisdom the preference. In recognition of this he was not only endowed with an understanding heart, but was given the means of acquiring great wealth, such as enabled him to build the most gorgeous of temples and the most sumptuous of palaces. The secret of Solomon's power was his possession of the Omnipotent Name engraved on his signet ring, the use of which he was to learn by an accident.

The first great problem Solomon was called upon to solve was how to build God's Temple in compliance with the unaccountable injunction not to employ iron implements in cutting, fitting, or smoothing the materials of the sacred edifice. This prohibition implied the existence of a rock splitting instrument of which neither the King nor his wisest counsellors had any knowledge. Eldad the lonely dweller of the sacred caves, the reader of the stars, the wanderer of the desert, the recorder of traditions, Eldad, who at the age of one hundred and nineteen years had no wrinkle on his face, preserving his faculties in all their strength by means of the occult sciences, this wizard who was the engraver of the Ineffable Name on the King's ring, was summoned to appear before His Majesty to answer this question.

"You know, Oh, Eldad, that I am to build the House of God with materials unprepared by the use of any iron implement. No doubt Providence has provided the means for the raising of His Sanctuary, but my advisers have failed to give me light on the mystery. Should it be beyond your power to enlighten me on this matter, I shall not know where to turn for the solution of the difficulty," spoke the King.

Eldad replied, "Know, Oh King, that in the beginning of things, as creation was nearing its completion, before the sun of the sixth day had withdrawn his last mellow beam from the earth, fourteen additional wonders were called into being, things which the foreknowledge of the All-knowing destined to play a part in this nether world. They are, the mouth of the earth that swallowed Korah and his rebellious followers, the mouth of the fountain known as Miriam's Well, the unfailing spring whose flow accompanied Israel through the desert, joining in the hymn of praise, the mouth of the brute that spoke to Balaam, after the heathen prophet had beaten it three times, he not having seen the angel that deterred it from advancing, the multi coloured rainbow which symbolizes God's mercy to frail man, the manna, Israel's food for forty years, the staff wherewith Moses performed all his miracles, the two sapphires out of which the tablets of the Law were cut, the gems that spelt the Ten Commandments, the letters of the alphabet, the sepulchre of Moses never seen by a mortal eye, the ram destined to be the substitute of Isaac when on the point of being sacrificed, the first pair of tongs, without which no iron could ever be forged, the spirits, both good and evil, the Sabbath having begun before bodies could be formed for some souls, thus left forever disembodied, and the Shamir, a worm not larger than a grain of barley, but stronger than rock, which it splits by the mere touch. The Shamir, Oh, King, is the only thing in creation to do the work in accordance with the divine behest. Those priceless gems of which the tablets and the letters thereon are cut have been fashioned by the Shamir."

"That Shamir shall be in my power, Oh, Eldad, it being there for the building of God's house, as it was there to materialize His immutable Word. But tell me who on earth claims possession of that wonderful creature? Is it to be had by trade, purchase, strategy, or force?" cried the King, deeply agitated.

"King, my knowledge goes no further than what I have told you. The abyss says, It is not in me, and the ocean says, I do not own it. Hitherto the Shamir has been beyond the reach of human eye. Whether it can be had, the future will tell. Here my wisdom ends," concluded the hoary wizard, withdrawing from the royal presence.

It was late in the evening when the King retired to a restless bed. Light and fitful as were his slumbers, his mind was haunted by weird visions of desolate scenes, cliffs infested with fierce carrion birds, and chasms teeming with venomous reptiles. The first blush of the morning found the monarch on one of his gilded balconies from which he surveyed the floral glories of his exuberant gardens, inhaling the odouriferous breezes of the peaceful morrow. Nature stood in her loveliness, and animate creation seemed to breathe peace. Suddenly there was a scream of pain in one of the towering clusters of green, and the next instant two specimens of the feathered tribes dropped at the feet of the King. In the talons of a carnivorous fowl was closed the tender wing of a trembling dove as white as snow. Moved by the impulse of pity, the King had his strong grip on the neck of the obscene bird of prey, relieving the other, but not before the victim's wing was broken. Great as was the anger of the King to see the poor dove bleeding and helpless, his astonishment was greater at the instantaneous transformation of the ferocious fowl in his grasp. The fowl was nothing other than a demon, black and mighty, swelling to enormous proportions, and beseeching the royal captor to set him free. "Whatever you bid me I will do, O, master, the ring on your finger giving you power over Ashmodai and his legions, to which I belong doing service as commanded," stated the dark agent submissively.

"And what cause underlies your vicious onslaught against so pure a creature as this dove?" asked Solomon, the revelation breaking on him that his signet ring invested him with a power akin to omnipotence.

"A symbol of purity, the dove comes under the ban of us who are of Ashmodai's dark legion," explained the fiend with unreserved candour.

"You shall not go there before I learn from you who keeps the Shamir," said Solomon firmly, assuming the demon to know something about it.

"What are you seeking of me, O, master, who am one of inferior rank bending to the will of our chief Ashmodai, the mighty spirit of this world? You must question him because he is the one to satisfy your demand," replied the demon.

"Describe his retreat to me and its approaches, and you shall go free," commanded the son of David.

"He is to be found where no creature of flesh and blood can long endure. It is not heaven, neither is it earth. Ashmodai's retreat is in the heart of the Orient, on the highest peak of the highest mountain range, in a hollow summit crowned with eternal snow, where, under a seal standing before a recess of frozen crystal, the purest spring under heaven flows to give him drink. Here he descends from his cloud vested realm, scans the seal to assure himself that no impurity has polluted his delicious beverage. When, having quenched his thirst, he re seals the fountain, he then gives audience to his court, who flock here to receive their orders, and refreshed by slumber he reascends to control the elements, and survey the work of his active host," was the information, which insured the demon's release.

In earnest consultation with his general Benaiah, Solomon matured the plan for the attack of Ashmodai's retreat, and before long a well-equipped expedition of a few picked men headed by that undaunted warrior, departed secretly. The haunt of the demoniac chief was not only far to the southeast of the Holy Land, but it was so located that in order to approach it the adventurers had to cross deserts, traverse pestiferous swamps infested with scorpions and dragons, ford wild rivers, and bridge over chasms, only to see themselves in a labyrinth of stupendous rocks, super mounted by a chain of sky towering peaks lost in dense fogs. Benaiah's eagle eye swept the clouded outlines of the snow-capped heights, trying in vain to locate the spot to be invaded. The impenetrable curtain of shifting fogs precluded accurate observation, and for once the dashing general felt that he was more in need of daring and of patience than of strategy. Retiring with his men to a cave at the base of the mountain, Benaiah took a position which commanded the loftiest point of the summit, hoping that something would occur to betray the object of his quest. Benaiah was struck by the contrast of the frowning mountain crest on one hand, and the sun's pure effulgence on the other. As he had his eyes riveted on the broken summit, the dense mass of fog darkened perceptibly. A noise as of a boisterous sea repelled by a rocky shore was the precursor of a tempest and an earthquake which convulsed the entire region within and without, thunder and lightning adding to the uproar. The eternal snows on the crest rose pulverized by the fury of a chaotic storm, a hurricane intermixed with flashes of red fire, the whole reducing itself within a few seconds to a funnel shaped whirlwind, revolving with furious speed, its pivot centred in a hollow betwixt mighty cliffs, rendered visible by the convulsive phenomenon. Benaiah knew what it meant, and he was confirmed in his assumption that Ashmodai was descending by observing the same disturbance a few hours later when the demon reascended to his airy empire.

Like a good strategist, the general took a little time to study the situation. The ascent of the mountain had to be made with great care, and the proceedings of the chief demon observed from as near a station as was compatible with safety. The climbing was attended with much toil and great danger, but the point was reached, the ground surveyed, and a hiding place secured in a recess barred by a wall of solid ice. Here everything was held in readiness for the next step.

If Ashmodai's descent startled the adventurers from a distance, nearness to the spot of his landing filled them with dismay, the atmospheric and subterranean agitation threatening to sweep them out of their hiding place. Like a thunderbolt striking to the centre of a hurricane, the demon shot down, unsealed his well, plunged his lips in the beryl fluid, drawing up a great quantity, and then sealed it up again. He was hardly ready when the table land around him was thick with files of demons, who arrived to report what had been accomplished, and to take orders for new tasks. They were all chiefs, of various ranks, each one having legions to carry out his behests. From the reports and the schemes discussed it was clear that they represented three kinds of spirits as to their relation to mankind of hostility, friendliness, and neutrality. There was a division of labour, hostile, benevolent, and neutral.

It is impossible to say how the daring band of interlopers would have fared at the hands of the terrible chief and his demonic army had not Benaiah possessed the Omnipotent Name to shield him from discovery. As matters stood the demons, unconscious of any unwelcome presence, departed, leaving Ashmodai to take his accustomed slumber, after which he darted up like a flash, with the phenomenal accompaniment of elemental disturbance as before. Now came Benaiah's opportunity. Without touching the seal on the cover of the well, the contents were drawn out through a hole skilfully bored beneath the surface of the liquid. This done, the hole was carefully closed, and another one was bored on the opposite side at a higher level, through which wine was poured to fill the emptied well. With every trace removed to avoid suspicion, and every detail ready for the emergency, Benaiah waited patiently for the next day.

Everything passed off as before, except for the astonishment of the dreaded power when he found that his well contained wine instead of water. Doomed by destiny to fall into the trap set for him, and urged by a parching thirst, Ashmodai took but little time to consider the advisability of drinking the intoxicating beverage, balancing Scriptural texts pro and con, and soon deciding to try its effect on his semi ethereal nature. This was just what Solomon and his general had counted on. Ashmodai had scarcely dismissed his military Council when the wine began to do its work, and he felt as he had never felt before, and he discussed with himself the singular mood in which he found himself plunged. He could not understand his new situation, the sensation being wholly new in his superhuman experience. Sleep was on him, and there he lay, stretched out as helpless as a senseless block. Benaiah was at hand with a chain rendered resistless by the Omnipotent Name engraved upon its links. Slipping it around the waist and the neck of the prince of demons, his potency was disposed of. Ashmodai's consternation when awakened words cannot describe. A roar of rage darkened all nature, shook the mountains to their foundation, and horrified all his legions who fled to hide themselves in the deepest chasms, even in the bowels of the earth and under the waters of the sea. For a moment Benaiah lost his speech, while his companions fell prostrate on the ground. The demon assumed every shape of horror to overawe the enemies of his freedom. In a few moments he gave himself the deterring shapes of all that is monstrous and deadly in nature, from the enraged tiger to the hissing serpent whose bite is death, all in vain.

"In the Name of the Highest, I, Benaiah, chief of King Solomon's army, do herewith command you, Ashmodai, mighty Prince of genii, to follow me to the seat of the wisest King, who needs your aid to build the Temple of God."

The conjuration conquered all resistance, and the demon was led off disarmed and humiliated. Realizing the hopelessness of gaining anything by violence, Ashmodai feigned submissiveness, assumed the form and manner of a most polished and affable courtier, and ushered into the presence of the King, charmed His Majesty by discourse of things far above the comprehension of ordinary men.

"You are to deliver to me the Shamir so that God's House be built without the use of iron implements," said Solomon to Ashmodai.

"The Shamir is not in my keeping, great King, the spirit of the ocean has entrusted it to the fowl Awza that it be preserved forever in a state of perfection," replied Ashmodai, adding, "and no man can come near that bird."

"Tell me where Awza breeds her young," commanded the King.

"South of the great desert there is a mountain with a towering cliff and walls so steep and smooth that a spider has difficulty to climb it. On the top of that rock is the nest of Awza, a fowl with claws of steel and eyes of fire, swift as the swallow, larger than the vulture, and fiercer than the eagle," answered the demon.

Again Benaiah was placed at the head of an expedition, and many were the hardships before the solitary pile rose before the eyes of the indomitable general. There was neither a bird to be seen nor a nest. The head of the precipitous rock was so high above the clouds that there seemed no possibility of scaling it. But Benaiah was full of resources and had anticipated the difficulty by bringing with him a pair of pigeons. Having left a man with the female bird this side of the mountain, the general made a detour for the opposite side with the male, tied a cord to his foot, and allowed him to rise. Guided by his instinct, the pigeon soon soared above the rock, descending to join his mate. This accomplished, a heavier cord was trailed over, followed by a still heavier rope strong enough to lift a man. This man was Benaiah who, in the dark of night, was hauled up by his attendants. Awza was thus to be circumvented.

Great was the general's joy when he found himself before the nest occupied by its fledglings, Awza being happily away in search for food. A transparent stone was laid securely over the nest. Awza arrived and found her fledglings imprisoned, hungry, and crying. With motherly tenderness she hurried to split the stone by applying the Shamir. Benaiah's great chance had come. From behind a boulder he burst forth and frightened the bird. She, in turn, dropped the invaluable worm. Benaiah pounced upon it like an eagle. The male bird was soon on the spot. A desperate struggle ensued between the enraged birds and the daring Benaiah. He was armed against iron claws and was not deterred by fiery eyes. He had the trophy and he held it, placing it in due time at the feet of his master, to the great surprise of Ashmodai. Thus was the building of God's Temple proceeded with, the Shamir splitting and fitting the materials.

Solomon's thirst for wisdom grew with his growing consciousness of the painful limitations as regards its acquisition by man, and Ashmodai availed himself of the King's avidity for knowledge in the hope of throwing him off his guard. He taught him the secrets of the vegetable and mineral kingdoms and gave him the clue to intercourse with animal creation, including the mind reading faculty. As a final achievement he suggested the weaving of a prodigious air float large enough to transport the King on his throne, an army fully equipped, and a host of spirits. On this air ship, sixty miles square, Solomon, ever accompanied by Ashmodai, traversed great distances, soaring above the clouds, higher than the eagle, and looking down on earth like a god. Woven by genii of the most subtle essences of nature, the texture of that air island was of azurean translucency, green blue in colour, floating in the sun's radiance like a rippled sea bathed in gold.

But the marvel of the marvellous equipage was its circular pavilion vast in extent and fashioned of rainbow tints, which photographed, enormously magnified, whatever came within the range of the eye that controlled its course, laying bare the mysteries of land and ocean, and revealing the multifarious activities of the spirit world under the rule of Ashmodai. Here Solomon's wonder throne, ascended by seven steps, each one guarded by a pair of magnificent animals chosen from the respective species of the lion, the elephant, the tiger, the bear, the serpent, the antelope, and the eagle, stood on a dais, lofty and brilliant, eclipsed only by the monarch's crown which rivalled the sun in splendour. Solomon began to believe that he was really more than human, and Ashmodai lost no chance to swell the autocrat's overbearing vanity. Solomon was so delighted with his triumph over the chief of demons and the deep secrets he had wrested from him, that he indefinitely deferred setting him free long after the Temple had been dedicated with grand ceremony, and, thanks to rock bursting Shamir, cargoes of gold were pouring into the royal treasury.

One early morning the sovereign of the richest kingdom upon earth bade the winds raise and waft his imponderable encampment toward the rising day, he being enthroned in his pavilion with Ashmodai at his feet. Up soared the magic float, lighter than air, transparent as ether, and stronger than adamant, hurrying eastward as an undulating firmament, suffused with purple and gold. The soundless vast above, coupled with the radiant flood that broke from the East, and the amazing kaleidoscope of animal and spirit life startlingly reflected by the walls of the glowing pavilion, overawed the mind of the most daring of kings, who exclaimed, "How great the all-powerful God, in whose infinity we are not more than an atom in the universe of matter!"

"Great King, your head is the microcosm of the immensity whose contemplation overpowers you. The heavens hide nothing which man cannot own if he but knew how," said Ashmodai with a pull at his chain.

"You are speaking riddles, potent spirit. Give me certainty that my grave is not the end, and your chains shall be broken," cried Solomon.

"King, disembodied you are my like, spirit of the everlasting Source, unchanged by change, but for the time dimmed, because engrossed with what is unethereal here. Yet even in your mortal coil I can give you, if restored to liberty, by virtue of your signet ring, a glimpse of things above your highest dreams, provided you will give me leave to stimulate your spiritual essence for the transmutation by harmony such as, at your bidding, I can cause my spirits to produce," promised Ashmodai.

"Then let the air vibrate with melody such as will fit my grosser substance for your suggested change," commanded Solomon, thoughtlessly.

At this the atmosphere trembled with the voices of a myriad chorus, throwing the King into an ecstasy of delight, ravishing his soul, and causing his tears to flow. In his ecstatic transport the monarch asked Ashmodai to come within the reach of his hand. A touch broke the chains of the wily demon, another movement of the hand delivered to him the signet ring and then the symphony sounded like the hissing of twenty thousand serpents, night swallowed the rays of the sun, a burst as of a hundred cannon shook the firmament, a tremendous pillar of lurid flame shot up into the height of azure, and from its core darted out a bundle that vanished beyond the sea. It was Solomon whom, by the might of his regained breath, Ashmodai had hurled to the end of earth, though allowing him to fall unhurt. The demon then dropped the ring into the deep. All this was the work of a moment, after which the atmosphere was clear and bright, the hissing ceased, and Solomon was on his throne. Or so it seemed. In reality it was Ashmodai in the guise of Solomon, robed in royalty to mock the power of the castaway autocrat.

Who would be wise enough to unmask the fraudulent usurper? Who would blame a spirit for avenging an outrageous humiliation? The court was informed that the chief of demons had escaped, and everything went on as before, including the tender attention due to the inmates of the royal harem.

Poor Solomon picked himself up in a far distant land, astonished and confused. His memory failed him, he stood transformed in face and form, and only darkly remembered that he had been a king somewhere. From his situation he could well infer that he had had some foolish dream of pomp and lordship. In reality he was a homeless beggar, shattered in health and unsound in mind. Starvation forced him to beg for bread, and vagabonds were his bed fellows in the wretched retreats open to the outcasts of humanity. His hours were divided between waking and dreaming, sane moments were followed by invasions of melancholy. Sometimes he doubted that his name was Solomon, that the world around him was real. A hard time was in store for the befooled wise man. Slowly the faculty of memory returned, and the singular circumstances which placed him where he found himself rose clearly before his recollection.

However, the knowledge of things immaterial which Solomon had acquired by his intimate intercourse with Ashmodai afforded him some help and comfort during his long wanderings from place to place, unhonoured, often the target of ridicule to such as heard him boast about his Solomonic pretensions. Great was his pain on hearing one day a strange traveller speak of the real Solomon's wisdom, his glorious rule, and the uncounted wealth that reached him by land and sea.

"Can it be that I am mad? If Solomon reigns in Jerusalem, who am I?" he asked himself, the confounded beggar king, and prayed humbly that he might be enlightened as to the nature of his condition. His pride was broken.

One late afternoon the royal wayfarer arrived, tired and hungry, before the gate of an inhospitable city. At first the unfriendly inhabitants denied him admission, but on hearing him claim the title of Solomon the Wise, they allowed his majesty to enter, convinced that they had a madman before them. Beyond this their hospitality did not extend. With a crust of bread as his supper, the unpitied monarch found no softer couch than the turf of a roofless enclosure, with many animals as his companions. The night was cold, and the situation tormenting for a starved man who had nothing wherewith to cover himself. After a few hours of restless slumber, Solomon felt his limbs so badly cramped that he was obliged to rise and walk to keep his blood in circulation. In the dimness of a clouded moon Solomon came near an old mare full of bruises, and so emaciated that one had no difficulty in counting her ribs. Solomon's experience rendered him accessible to sympathy with life in misery, and he derived sad consolation from the sight of other creatures who were even more wretched than he. He reflected that man is the source of great torments and wretchedness here below in inflicting pain on creatures entrusted him by a kind Providence.

It was about midnight when the royal beggar rose again to renew his walk, finding it impossible to drown his worry in oblivious sleep. The moon shone brightly, and the deep silence held the weird landscape in magic repose, forming a strong contrast with the agitation suppressed in the king's bosom. Presently familiar notes fell on Solomon's ear, it was the speech of the ill-fated mare, who spoke words of sorrow to her inexperienced family, giving them her maternal advice now that her end was near. With bated breath the man listened to the story of a lifelong agony, recited by a creature of the noblest species under human control.

"Yes, I have often been whipped and kicked by my cruel master. Ah, hunger, too, and thirst, the heat by day and the cold by night, I endured, toiling, toiling under the rod, and now that I am old he has turned me out that I perish unsheltered, unfed. Too weak am I to drive off the flies which torture me, and death will not come. Once I was led to believe that we horses had an advantage over the animals that are slaughtered for food. The sight of a victim's blood shed by the carnivorous lust of man made me shudder. I have seen the head of the fowl twisted off, have seen lambs swim in their blood, have seen the calf taken for slaughter from the side of her dam who rent the air with lamentation, have seen cattle felled by the deadly club in the hand of gluttonous man. And have I not, in my younger days, been used in the chase? Mounted on me, my master, in company of his like, thought it great sport to unleash a pack of bloody hounds in pursuit of a frightened hare, fox, or deer. Hunted down, the agonized creatures fell, to be torn to pieces. Man is our devil, helpless, dumb animals that we are. Enough is there in nature to glut his hunger. The hen supplies him with her eggs, the cow with her milk and with butter and cheese, and the lamb with its wool, while we carry him and his burdens, multiply his strength in battle, and gratify his love of pomp and pleasure. Honey, fruits, mushrooms, and a variety of grains and vegetables should protect animate creation from his deathful greed."

"There will be a dead fellow tomorrow," said a lusty colt made hot by his dam's tale of woe. "That master of yours will not long be master of mine, one kick of my hind legs will do for him, let him try it with me, he won't whip me a second time."

"Child, never try it, if you love me," cried the intelligent, but much abused mare. "A vicious horse, as they brand one who resents abuse, is sure to get his double share of torture, I have tried it and had the worst of it. Kick your master once and his vengeance will take years to bleed you to death."

"But I won't stand it. I will kick right and left, break windows, bones, vehicles, break whatever comes in my way, and break myself if it must be. They will be kept busy watching my legs, I won't stand it," answered the colt determinedly.

"You may as well kick against a rock and have your hind legs broken, or throw yourself into a millpond and be drowned, as seek revenge by hurting your master. We are not unavenged, however. Nature, our common mother, does not allow her offenders to go unpunished. If man would simply be content to live on what the animal and vegetable kingdoms freely give him, he would be a much happier, tamer, healthier and nobler being. Chase and slaughter create that ferocious temper which revels in bloodshed, so that his own kindred bleed, victims of his atrocity. Child, I, too, have revolted in my time. Exasperated by the cuts of a whip in the hand of a miscreant, I once made a wild break for deliverance, fled madly through the street, dashed against everything in my way, dashed against a throng of men, women, and children, who tried vainly to escape, did all the harm I could, and landed bruised and breathless among the terrified children in an open schoolyard, killing one and hurting others. Thereafter I was treated as the savage beast, was kicked in and out of time, my legs being fettered and my head held fast by a chain tied to the wall. When employed, the bit in my mouth was cruelly tight, and that was all I gained. A higher will must have decreed this to be our lot," concluded the starving mare, lowering her head mournfully.

Solomon, whom the equine group had not noticed, approached, and astonished them by addressing them in the language they so well understood. The luckless mare raised her head, and her glazed eyes flashed as the soft voice of the king said, "You are right, Oh, noble creature, in charging your master with unkindness and ingratitude toward your high-spirited race that has rendered him invaluable service. Yes, man is as yet a child and a slave of habit but will in due time rise to an understanding of his duties toward the myriad lives around him, not created for wanton abuse or ruthless destruction. Indeed, he pays dearly for the gratification of his lower instincts, the benign Creator having meant him to be prompted by the gentler, deeper, sweeter qualities of his being. The day will come when he shudders at the idea of sustaining his life by the immolation of others, when the flesh eater will be seen in the same light as the cannibal. My name is Solomon, and in my kingdom they called me The Wise, but my wisdom fails to enlighten me why things are as they are when they could be so much better. Believe me, man has tortures of body and soul, and has, like you, his devil to plague and circumvent him. Holy Writ contains beautiful words in praise of the horse, he, armed with thunder, nobler than the lion, fearless as the eagle, graceful as the zebra, strong as the wave, quick as the wind, the pride of the warrior, the pleasure of the prince, the seat of the king. Once restored to power, I will remember the burden of your grievance, faithful mare, and your race will be benefited as far as my will shall prevail."

The horses were pleased with the sympathetic words of their distinguished friend, and the ambitious colt offered to carry him as far as he wished. Solomon had plenty of leisure to explain the difficulty into which he had been plunged by the wiles of Ashmodai, and that he was sure of restoration the moment he could enter the gates of his beloved Jerusalem.

"May your wisdom, your kindness and your kingdom spread far and wide, Oh, King! so that my helpless offsprings be spared the torments that I have endured during the length of my days!" prayed the mare, with a tremor which betrayed extreme weakness. The next instant saw the poor brute tremble, stagger, fall and expire.

If Solomon had counted on an easy triumph over his formidable adversary, his arrival at Jerusalem, after years of told hardships and trials, undeceived him. The city showed every indication of great prosperity, the kingdom stood firmly established, and the brilliance of the royal Court had no rival in the gorgeous Orient. Embassies came to pay the homage of princedoms and empires near and far, bringing presents of rare animals, gold, costly products, and precious stones, and they departed overawed by the superhuman wisdom of Israel's mighty ruler, who amazed the ambassadors not alone by addressing each one in his native language but by showing a minute acquaintance with their secret matters of state, and by reading their hidden thoughts. The envoys reported to their sovereigns that a demigod had come to reign over an earthly kingdom.

For a shabby mendicant to overthrow a power of Ashmodai's devices and resources was indeed a business to make even a Solomon despair of success.

Having entered the city, the beggar king sought the haunts of the paupers without breathing a syllable as to his identity, lest Ashmodai be alarmed by his presence, which was a circumstance to be feared. Solomon the beggar knew that he looked so unlike Solomon the Wise that he hesitated for a long time before approaching his faithful Benaiah, who, innocent of the demon's fraud, continued as dashing and as loyal as ever before.

The attempt at an interview resulted in the general's throwing a silver coin to get rid of the importunate beggar, who dared accost him as though he was his equal. In his despondency Solomon turned his back on his endeared capital, roamed about for many days distracted with grief, until, having caught sight of the sea, he fell prostrate on the shore, prayed in great humility, wept, and fell asleep. He had a dream in which Eldad, who had died during his wanderings, appeared to him in the guise of an angler, unloosening a large fish from his hook which he presented to the dreamer. A scream in the air startled Solomon from his sleep, and a slap on his cheek by some cold thing brought him to his feet. Before him lay a fish in contortions, while above him two birds were soaring, one higher than the other, who, in their fight for the prey, evidently had allowed it to drop on the sleeper's face. Parched with thirst and stung by hunger, Solomon tore the fish open, when, the ring, Eldad's gift, the all-controlling charm, was there. No sooner was it on the King's finger than an appalling earthquake shook the shore, while from the heart of God's city burst a prodigious pillar of smoke and flame, losing itself in the deep azure. Useless to add that this was the trail of Ashmodai's precipitous flight, who, immediately apprised of his adversary's triumph, fled as fast as he could, spreading consternation as he went.

Solomon by this time had enough experience with the chief of demons to last him for the rest of his life, yet nothing else but Ashmodai's subsequent vengeance was the cause of his falling from grace in after years, so that the wisest of ancient kings not alone forfeited the power vested in the Omnipotent Name, but closed a glorious career so ingloriously that he died an object of pity to some of his subjects and of hatred to the rest. Having secured the means of building the Temple without the aid of ordinary implements, he would have acted wisely in dismissing the chief of invisible hosts instead of detaining him unjustly and prying into mysteries not intended for man. Solomon's aspiration to be more than human, while it gratified his vanity, brought on eventually his ruin, while his mind was never at ease, even under the constant guardianship of the *Heroic Sixty*, his close bodyguard.

Historical Notes

This section contains some brief biographical notes about the original collectors and their books featured in this collection. These notes have been adapted from those primarily on Wikipedia along with other supporting sources and notes.

Abraham G. Seklemian

Abraham G. Seklemian (1870–1958) was a prominent Armenian-American writer, educator, and community leader, known for his significant contributions to Armenian literature and culture in the United States. Born in Kharpert, Ottoman Empire (now Harput, Turkey), Seklemian immigrated to the United States in the late 19th century, seeking refuge from the persecution and violence targeting Armenians in the Ottoman Empire.

Upon arriving in the United States, Seklemian became deeply involved in the Armenian-American community, dedicating his life to preserving Armenian heritage and advancing the interests of his people. He played a pivotal role in establishing Armenian cultural institutions and organizations across the country, serving as a bridge between Armenian immigrants and their new homeland while fostering a sense of unity and solidarity within the diaspora.

Seklemian's literary contributions were instrumental in shaping Armenian-American identity and preserving Armenian culture for future generations. He was a prolific writer, poet, and editor, whose works explored themes of Armenian history, folklore, and identity. His writings often reflected the struggles and triumphs of the Armenian people, serving as a testament to their resilience and perseverance in the face of adversity.

One of Seklemian's most notable achievements was his role as the editor of the Armenian Mirror-Spectator, a prominent Armenian-American newspaper based in Massachusetts. Under his leadership, the newspaper became a vital platform for disseminating news, literature, and cultural content to the Armenian diaspora in the United States, fostering a sense of community and solidarity among Armenians across the country.

In addition to his literary pursuits, Seklemian was also a dedicated educator, committed to providing Armenian-American youth with access to quality education and cultural enrichment. He played a key role in the establishment of Armenian schools and educational programs, helping to preserve the Armenian language and instil a sense of pride in Armenian heritage among younger generations.

Throughout his life, Abraham G. Seklemian remained a tireless advocate for the Armenian cause, tirelessly lobbying for recognition of the Armenian Genocide and working to raise awareness about the plight of the Armenian people. His contributions to Armenian literature, culture, and community-building continue to be celebrated and revered within the Armenian diaspora, ensuring that his legacy lives on for generations to come.

Henry Wysham Lanier

Henry Wysham Lanier (1873–1937) was an American author, biographer, and editor, known for his significant contributions to literature and his insightful biographical works. Born in Baltimore, Maryland, in 1873, Lanier was the son of Sidney Lanier, a renowned American poet, musician, and author.

Growing up in a literary household, Henry Wysham Lanier developed a deep appreciation for literature and the arts from an early age. He inherited his father's passion for storytelling and embarked on a career in writing and publishing, following in the footsteps of his esteemed parent.

Lanier's literary pursuits encompassed various genres, including fiction, non-fiction, and biography. He displayed a particular interest in the lives and works of notable literary figures, which became a focal point of his writing career. Lanier's biographical works provided insightful portraits of writers such as Edgar Allan Poe, Walt Whitman, and others, shedding light on their personal lives, creative processes, and literary legacies.

In addition to his own writing, Lanier made significant contributions as an editor and compiler of literary anthologies. He curated collections of poetry and prose, showcasing the diverse voices and talents within the American literary landscape. Lanier's editorial efforts helped to popularize and preserve works of literature for future generations, ensuring their continued relevance and appreciation.

Throughout his career, Henry Wysham Lanier maintained a commitment to literary scholarship and cultural preservation. His meticulous research and nuanced portrayals of literary figures earned him recognition as a respected authority in the field of

American literature. Lanier's writings were praised for their depth of insight, clarity of expression, and appreciation for the richness of the human experience.

Beyond his literary endeavours, Lanier was also actively involved in various cultural and educational initiatives. He participated in literary societies, lectured on literature and the arts, and engaged in community-building efforts that promoted the importance of literature and cultural heritage.

Henry Wysham Lanier's legacy endures through his writings, which continue to inspire and enlighten readers interested in American literature and literary biography. His dedication to understanding and celebrating the lives of writers has left an indelible mark on the literary landscape, ensuring that the contributions of these literary giants are remembered and cherished for years to come.

Louis A. Boettiger

When Louis Angelo Boettiger was born on 3 July 1891, in Chicago, Cook, Illinois, United States, his father, Adam Charles Boettiger, was 25 and his mother, Emma Dralle, was 20. He lived in Wisconsin, United States in 1962. He died on 12 March 1962, in Appleton, Outagamie, Wisconsin, United States, at the age of 70.

Louis A. Boettiger wrote a book called *Armenian Legends and Festivals*, where he dives deep into Armenian culture and traditions. He explores the stories and celebrations that have been a part of Armenian identity for centuries. Even though we don't know much about Boettiger himself, his work shows how much he cares about Armenian heritage and wants to make sure it's remembered. *Armenian Legends and Festivals* isn't just a dry academic book, it's full of fascinating myths and customs that bring Armenian culture to life. Boettiger's writing is clear and interesting, making these ancient stories accessible to everyone, not just experts. This book isn't just for Armenians, it's for anyone who loves history, mythology, and learning about different cultures.

Gertrude Landa

Gertrude Landa (1867–1951) was a prolific English author, translator, and advocate for Jewish culture. Born in London in 1867, Landa demonstrated a passion for literature and language from an early age. She embarked on a literary career that would span several decades and leave a lasting impact on children's literature and the preservation of Jewish heritage.

Landa's interest in Jewish culture led her to become a prominent figure in the Jewish literary community of her time. She was deeply engaged in the study and promotion of Jewish folklore, traditions, and literature. Her dedication to preserving Jewish heritage led her to explore Yiddish literature, which she translated into English, thereby making it accessible to a broader audience.

Throughout her career, Landa authored numerous books, many of which were aimed at children. Her works often featured Jewish themes, stories, and characters, reflecting her commitment to celebrating and preserving Jewish culture. Landa's writings appealed not only to Jewish audiences but also to readers of diverse backgrounds, contributing to a greater understanding and appreciation of Jewish heritage.

One of Landa's notable contributions was her role as a translator of Yiddish literature into English. Through her translations, she introduced English-speaking audiences to the rich tapestry of Yiddish storytelling, folklore, and poetry. Her translations helped bridge cultural divides and fostered greater awareness and appreciation of Jewish literary traditions.

In addition to her literary endeavours, Landa was actively involved in various philanthropic and educational initiatives within the Jewish community. She believed in the importance of education and cultural preservation, and her advocacy work reflected these values.

Gertrude Landa's legacy lives on through her writings, translations, and advocacy for Jewish culture. Her contributions to children's literature and her efforts to preserve and promote Jewish heritage continue to inspire readers and scholars alike. Landa's dedication to literature, language, and cultural preservation left an indelible mark on the literary landscape of her time and continues to resonate with audiences today.

James Johonnot

James Johonnot (1823–1888) was an American educator, author, and advocate for educational reform, known for his significant contributions to the field of education during the 19th century. Born on September 6, 1823, in Chateaugay, New York, Johonnot's early experiences instilled in him a passion for learning and teaching that would shape his career.

After completing his own education, Johonnot embarked on a teaching career, working in schools throughout New York and Michigan. He quickly distinguished himself as an innovative educator, implementing progressive teaching methods and advocating for a more practical and experiential approach to learning.

Johonnot's interest in educational reform led him to become involved in various educational organizations and initiatives. He served as a superintendent of schools in several Michigan communities, where he worked to improve educational standards and expand access to schooling for all children.

Throughout his career, Johonnot authored numerous textbooks and educational resources, many of which became widely used in schools across the United States. His books covered a wide range of subjects, including history, geography, science, and literature, and were praised for their clarity, accuracy, and engaging style.

One of Johonnot's most influential works was *Geographical Reader for the Dixie Children*, published in 1879. This geography textbook aimed to provide students with a comprehensive understanding of the world around them, incorporating vivid descriptions, illustrations, and maps to bring geographical concepts to life.

In addition to his work as an author and educator, Johonnot was also a fervent advocate for the advancement of women's education. He believed strongly in the importance of providing equal educational opportunities for all, regardless of gender, and worked tirelessly to promote the education and empowerment of women.

James Johonnot's dedication to educational excellence and reform left a lasting impact on the field of education in the United States. His progressive ideas and innovative teaching methods helped to shape the way education was approached in the 19th century and laid the groundwork for future developments in the field. Johonnot's legacy continues to be celebrated by educators and scholars alike, as his contributions to education remain relevant and influential to this day.

Ohannes Chatschumian

Ohannes Chatschumian (1851–1927) was a notable Armenian writer, educator, and public figure, celebrated for his contributions to Armenian literature and culture during the late 19th and early 20th centuries. Born in Constantinople (modern-day Istanbul) in 1851,

Chatschumian grew up amidst the vibrant cultural and intellectual milieu of the Armenian community in the Ottoman Empire.

From an early age, Chatschumian displayed a keen interest in literature and language, laying the foundation for a lifelong commitment to literary pursuits. He received a traditional Armenian education before furthering his studies in Constantinople, where he immersed himself in Armenian and European literature, philosophy, and history.

Chatschumian's literary career began in earnest during the late 19th century when he emerged as a prominent voice in Armenian literature. He was a prolific writer, producing poetry, prose, essays, and translations that reflected his deep love for Armenian language and culture. His works often explored themes of identity, nationalism, and the Armenian experience, resonating deeply with readers both within and outside the Armenian community.

In addition to his literary endeavours, Chatschumian was also actively involved in educational initiatives aimed at preserving and promoting Armenian culture. He served as a teacher and educator, dedicating himself to the intellectual and moral development of Armenian youth. Through his teaching and mentorship, Chatschumian inspired a new generation of Armenian writers and intellectuals, leaving an indelible mark on Armenian literary and educational circles.

One of Chatschumian's most notable achievements was his role in the founding of literary and cultural journals, which served as important platforms for Armenian writers and thinkers to exchange ideas and engage in intellectual discourse. He contributed essays, articles, and editorials to these publications, using his platform to advocate for social reform, cultural revival, and national unity among Armenians.

Despite facing numerous challenges and setbacks throughout his life, including political persecution and censorship, Chatschumian remained steadfast in his commitment to the Armenian cause. He continued to write and publish works of literature and scholarship that celebrated the richness of Armenian culture and affirmed the resilience of the Armenian people.

Ohannes Chatschumian's legacy as a writer, educator, and cultural figure continues to be celebrated within the Armenian community and beyond. His literary contributions, marked by their depth of thought, artistic sensibility, and unwavering commitment to Armenian identity, remain an enduring source of inspiration for generations of Armenian writers, scholars, and cultural activists.

Miss Alice Fletcher

Miss Alice Fletcher (1838–1923) was a pioneering American ethnologist, anthropologist, and advocate for Native American rights, known for her ground-breaking work in documenting and preserving First Nation culture and heritage during the late 19th and early 20th centuries. Born on March 15, 1838, in Cuba, New York, Alice Fletcher's early life was marked by a deep curiosity about the world around her and a passion for social justice.

Fletcher's interest in First Nation cultures was sparked during her childhood, when she encountered First Nation artifacts and stories while exploring the countryside near her home. This early fascination with indigenous peoples would shape her future career and become the focus of her life's work.

After receiving a formal education, Fletcher embarked on a career as an ethnologist and anthropologist, specializing in the study of

First Nation cultures. She travelled extensively throughout the United States, conducting fieldwork and research among various Indigenous tribes, including the Omaha, Sioux, and Nez Perce peoples.

One of Fletcher's most significant contributions to the field of anthropology was her pioneering use of ethnographic methods to document First Nation lifeways and traditions. She collaborated closely with indigenous communities, forging strong relationships based on mutual respect and trust, and worked tirelessly to record and preserve their languages, rituals, and customs for future generations.

Fletcher's advocacy for First Nation rights was integral to her work as an ethnologist. She recognized the injustices and hardships faced by Indigenous peoples as a result of colonialism and government policies, and she dedicated herself to advocating for their rights and dignity. Fletcher played a key role in the establishment of the Indian Rights Association, an organization dedicated to protecting the rights of First Nation peoples and advocating for reforms in government Indian policies.

In addition to her scholarly pursuits and advocacy work, Fletcher was also a prolific writer and lecturer, publishing numerous articles, books, and papers on First Nation culture and anthropology. Her writings helped to popularize the field of ethnology and raise awareness about the richness and diversity of Indigenous cultures.

Alice Fletcher's legacy as a pioneering ethnologist and advocate for First Nation rights continues to be celebrated today. Her contributions to the preservation of indigenous cultures and the advancement of indigenous rights laid the groundwork for future generations of anthropologists and activists, leaving an indelible mark on the field of anthropology and the ongoing struggle for indigenous sovereignty and self-determination.

Charlotte Mary Yonge

Charlotte Mary Yonge (1823–1901) was a prolific English novelist, best known for her significant contributions to Victorian literature, particularly in the realm of historical fiction and children's literature. Born on August 11, 1823, in Otterbourne, Hampshire, Charlotte Yonge grew up in a devout Anglican family, where she developed a deep appreciation for literature and education.

Yonge's literary career began in earnest with the publication of her first novel, *Abbeychurch*, in 1844. This marked the beginning of a prolific writing career that spanned over six decades and produced over 160 works, including novels, short stories, essays, and educational literature

One of Yonge's most enduring legacies is her contributions to children's literature. She authored numerous novels and stories aimed at young readers, imbuing her tales with moral lessons, Christian values, and historical context. Her works, including *The Daisy Chai*n (1856) and *The Little Duke* (1854), captivated young audiences and became beloved classics of children's literature.

In addition to her children's literature, Yonge was also celebrated for her historical fiction, which often depicted English history through vivid characters and rich narrative detail. Her novels, such as *The Heir of Redclyffe* (1853) and *Heartsease* (1854), enjoyed widespread popularity and critical acclaim, establishing Yonge as one of the leading novelists of the Victorian era.

Beyond her literary pursuits, Charlotte Yonge was deeply committed to philanthropy and social reform. She was actively involved in various charitable endeavours, including educational initiatives for women and the promotion of literacy among the working class. Yonge's advocacy for social causes reflected her belief in the power of literature to effect positive change and inspire moral virtue.

Throughout her life, Charlotte Yonge remained dedicated to her writing, producing a vast body of work that continues to be celebrated for its moral depth, historical accuracy, and literary craftsmanship. Her novels and stories have left an indelible mark on English literature, influencing subsequent generations of writers and readers alike.

Charlotte Mary Yonge passed away on March 24, 1901, leaving behind a rich literary legacy that continues to be cherished and admired by readers around the world. Her contributions to Victorian literature and children's literature have ensured her lasting place in the pantheon of English literary greats.

Henry Iliowizi

Henry Iliowizi, also known as Henry Iliowizi Ben-Israel or Henry Iliowizi Cohen, was an American musician, composer, and conductor, best known for his contributions to Jewish music during the early 20th century. Born in the late 19th century, Iliowizi was a prominent figure in the Jewish musical community, particularly in New York City.

Iliowizi was a versatile musician, skilled in both classical and traditional Jewish music. He was known for his ability to blend elements of European classical music with Jewish melodies and themes, creating compositions that resonated deeply with Jewish audiences.

One of Iliowizi's most notable achievements was his work as a conductor and arranger. He conducted orchestras and ensembles, performing both classical repertoire and his own compositions. His arrangements of Jewish liturgical music and folk songs helped to popularize Jewish music within the broader musical community.

In addition to his work as a conductor, Iliowizi was also a prolific composer. He wrote numerous pieces for orchestra, chamber ensemble, and voice, many of which were inspired by Jewish themes and traditions. His compositions ranged from solemn liturgical music to lively folk dances, showcasing the breadth and diversity of Jewish musical expression.

Iliowizi's contributions to Jewish music were widely recognized during his lifetime, and his legacy continues to be celebrated today. His compositions and arrangements remain an important part of the Jewish musical canon, and his pioneering efforts to blend classical and Jewish musical traditions have had a lasting impact on Jewish music around the world.

In addition to his musical output, Henry Iliowizi also contributed to *The Weird Orient*, a collection of short stories edited by Henry Iliowizi and H. P. Lovecraft, published in 1930. The other contributors to this book include:

- H. P. Lovecraft: An American writer known for his contributions to the horror genre, particularly for his creation of the Cthulhu Mythos.
- Thomas Burke: A British author best known for his *Limehouse Nights* stories, which explore the lives of London's Chinese community.
- Farnsworth Wright: An American writer and editor who served as the editor of *Weird Tales* magazine, where many of the stories in *The Weird Orient* were originally published.

- C. M. Eddy Jr.: An American author known for his contributions to pulp fiction and his collaborations with H. P. Lovecraft.
- Charles R. Tanner: An American author whose work often explored exotic locales and supernatural themes.
- Arthur J. Burks: An American writer known for his prolific output of pulp fiction, including many stories featuring supernatural and adventure themes.

These contributors each provided stories that fit the theme of the anthology, offering readers a glimpse into the strange and mysterious world of the Orient through the lens of speculative fiction and horror.

About The Editor

Born in 1962 into a household that lived and breathed sports, the editor's dad was a seasoned senior amateur and lower league professional footballer. Not just that, he managed his own businesses in cahoots with Clive's mum, who was no slouch either – she was a skilled and award-winning dancer.

After snagging a degree in History from Leeds University, our storyteller took a rather serendipitous stroll into the burgeoning world of information technology in the late '80s. Like father, like son, they say. Alongside a flourishing tech career, Clive dabbled in various writing and acting pursuits, from freelancing as a journalist and book reviewer (with a coveted by-line in The Sunday People) to gracing stages in village halls and even professional theatres all across the south of the UK for a good decade.

In a nod to the family's sporting legacy, Clive - long after hanging up his own boots - delved into the world of live TV broadcasts. Armed with a wealth of rugby knowledge, he became one of the go-to 'statos' for the BBC, ITV, TVNZ, and EuroSport, covering everything from Heineken Cups to Six Nations, World Sevens, and World Cups in the late '90s.

For a deeper dive into this fascinating journey, head over to clivegilson.com, where there's a whole trove of tales waiting to be uncovered!